OUTNUMBERED . . .

Clint started toward the house with his hands held away from his body. He didn't think Billy the Kid would shoot an unarmed man, but he tensed just the same. As he reached the front porch, the door opened and McSween appeared. Clint entered and closed the door. Immediately, ten guns were on him.

"Billy?" Clint asked, looking at the Kid.

"You know me?"

"Only by sight," Clint said. "From descriptions."

"Well," Billy said, "I've heard of you, but I ain't never seen you. So you're the Gunsmith, huh?"

"That's right."

"Bet you ain't too comfortable with that empty holster."

Billy held his own gun loosely in his hand. The two men stared at each other for a few moments, then Billy holstered his gun. The other men, however, covered him.

"You can take Mrs. McSween. What else?"

"Well," Clint said, "I was kind of hoping you'd give yourself up. There's forty men out there, and there's probably going to be some help coming from Fort Sumner . . ."

THE GUNSMITH

THE GHOST OF BILLY THE KID

J. R. ROBERTS

JOVE BOOKS, NEW YORK

This is a work of fiction. Names, characters, places, and incidents either are the product of the author's imagination or are used fictitiously, and any resemblance to actual persons, living or dead, business establishments, events, or locales is entirely coincidental.

THE GHOST OF BILLY THE KID

A Jove Book / published by arrangement with
the author

PRINTING HISTORY
Jove edition / October 2003

Copyright © 2003 by Robert J. Randisi

ISBN: 0-515-13622-0

A JOVE BOOK®
Jove Books are published by The Berkley Publishing Group,
a division of Penguin Group (USA) Inc.,
375 Hudson Street, New York, New York 10014.
JOVE and the "J" design
are trademarks belonging to Penguin Group (USA) Inc.

PRINTED IN THE UNITED STATES OF AMERICA

10 9 8 7 6 5 4 3 2 1

THE GHOST OF BILLY THE KID

ONE

When Clint Adams rode into White Oaks, New Mexico, he didn't know what to expect. What he didn't expect was that it had become a ghost town.

Well, not exactly a ghost town. There were people living there, but it had nowhere near the population it had the first time he was there, years before.

"What happened here?" he asked aloud, as he rode Eclipse down the main street. Gold had been discovered here in 1879, in the nearby Jicarilla Mountains, and the town had boomed. Not only gold, but coal, as well. White Oaks was in the midst of its boom when he first rode in and rode down this same street. Today he was riding Eclipse, the Darley Arabian given him by showman P. T. Barnum. Back then, however, he'd been riding his big black gelding, Duke.

He patted Eclipse's neck and said, "Boom's over, I guess."

The same buildings were there, but some were in a sad

state of disrepair. He rode Eclipse up to the White Oaks Saloon and dismounted. He paused as he stepped up onto the boardwalk in front of the saloon and looked around. There was activity, but nothing like the hustle and bustle of years gone by. Even the light breeze that blew down the street and onto his face felt lonely.

He turned and went into the saloon. The heads of three men turned to stare at him as he entered, then turned back. The bartender looked over at him, and leaned on the bar and waited for him to approach. For the life of him Clint couldn't recall if this was the same bartender as the last time he was there, but that didn't really matter.

"What can I get ya?" the bartender asked. He was tall, dark-haired, with a nose so big Clint thought he would have remembered it. He decided this man had not been here the last time he had.

"Beer."

The bartender filled a mug, with only about a half inch of foam on top, and set it down in front of him.

"Thanks."

Clint took a sip and set it down. It was lukewarm.

"Town's got quiet," he said.

"You been here before?"

"A while back."

"Before or after Billy?"

"What?"

"Before or after Billy the Kid got killed?"

"Uh . . . before. Why?"

"Town got quiet after Billy got killed."

"Really?" Clint asked. "So . . . the mines haven't petered out?"

"Not that I know of," the barman said. "Not yet, anyway."

"I see."

Of course, Clint knew the story of Pat Garrett killing Billy the Kid in nearby Fort Sumner. He had no idea, though, that the Kid's death could have this effect on a town.

"Is the Little Casino still open?"

"Sure. Down the street—"

"I know where it is. Still run by Belle La Mar?"

"Madam Varnish? Sure. Hey, everything's kinda the same, it just ain't, ya know, a real lively place no more."

"Because Billy got killed."

"Right."

"But . . . that was a while ago."

"Hey, ya know," the barman said, "that war ain't ever over."

He was speaking of the Lincoln County War, otherwise known as the Five Day War. His last visit had taken place well before the "war," and yet he had always wondered what effect his presence might have had on that war. Also, what might have happened if he'd stayed long enough to be involved?

"Damn Pat Garrett," someone muttered from behind.

Clint turned and said, "Pardon me?"

One of the men looked up and stared at Clint blearily.

"I said damn Pat Garrett," he repeated. "Somebody should put a bullet in him."

"I thought he was doing his job."

"If your job is killin' your best friend, he was," the bartender said.

"Billy was a killer," one of the other men said, "and Garrett was the law."

"You hush up, Phillips," the barman said.

"Yeah, shut yer damn yap, Phil," the first man said.

"Whyn't you come and shut it fer me, Cork."

The first man started to get up and the barman yelled, "Not in my place, damn it! You fellas want to keep fightin' the damn Lincoln County War, take it outside."

The two men glared at each other, and then apparently decided it was more important to finish their drink.

Clint turned back to the bartender and ignored the luke-warm beer.

"Everybody around here feel like that?"

"Everybody took sides," the bartender said. "Some was for Murphy, and some was for Tunstall and McSween. Some was for Billy, and some for Garrett."

"What about you?"

The bartender shrugged and said, "Whatever's good for business."

Clint decided not to tell the man that cold beer might be good for business. He tossed a coin on the bar and said, "Thanks."

"Stayin' long?" the bartender asked.

"Don't know," Clint said. "I hope not."

TWO

Clint retrieved Eclipse from in front of the White Oaks Saloon and decided to walk the horse down to the Little Casino. He'd met Belle La Mar last time, but had spent time with one of the girls who worked for Belle. Nothing had happened between him and Belle, but there had been some attraction there. Of course, she had not been a very young woman then, so he was curious to see what she looked like now.

She had gotten her nickname, "Madam Varnish," because of the slick way she did business. She had a partner, but virtually ran both the gambling and the girls in her place.

Once again Clint left Eclipse outside as he entered Belle La Mar's Little Casino.

It was midday, so the gambling tables were mostly covered, except for a poker game going on in one corner. The five players all looked listless, and the pot looked small.

Clint turned and walked to the bar, hoping that this time the beer would be cold.

"Beer," he said to the barkeep before the man could speak. "A cold one."

"Only kind we got," the bartender said, setting it in front of him. "Belle wouldn't have it no other way." This barman was beefy, with large forearms and sloping shoulders. Clint was sure he doubled as the bouncer.

"Where is Belle?" Clint asked. He sipped the beer and it was ice cold. He took another swallow and savored the feel of it as it slid down his throat.

"You got business with Belle?"

"No," Clint said. "Pleasure."

"We got other girls for that," the man said. "Belle don't do that—"

"Take it easy, fella," Clint said. "I'm just an old friend riding through town. Thought I'd stop and say hello."

"What's your name?" the bartender asked, eyeing him suspiciously.

"Adams, Clint Adams."

"Hey," the man said, then, "hey" again, as he took a step back, obviously recognizing the name. "I didn't mean nothing, Mr. Adams—"

"Relax," Clint said. "I just want to see Belle."

"Sure thing, Mr. Adams," the bartender said. "I'll just go and fetch her for you."

"There's no need to rush—" Clint started, but the bartender had already run out from behind the bar and taken off toward the back of the room. Some of the customers looked after him curiously, then over at Clint, who busied himself finishing the cold beer.

When the bartender returned, Madam Varnish was trailing behind him. Time, as it turned out, had not been kind to her. Never a tall woman, she had put on enough weight to make her look even shorter. Her face was covered with powder and rouge to cover whatever time had done to her skin, and her still deep cleavage had some wrinkles in it. Her eyes, however, sparkled when she saw Clint and she hugged him tightly to her. The perfume she was wearing was so strong his eyes were threatening to tear.

"Clint Adams, goddammit," she said. "Where have you been all these years?"

"Hello, Belle," he said. "Well, I've—"

"Never mind," she said, releasing him and standing away at arm's length. "I've read about all your exploits since I saw you last. You've become even more famous than our own Billy." She spoke the name of William Bonney, alias Billy the Kid, with great affection.

"Did you have a beer?" she demanded.

"I had one, yes—"

"Have another," she said. "Clarence, another beer for my friend and don't you dare charge him while he's in town."

"No, ma'am," the bartender said, and then, "I mean, yes, ma'am."

"Grab your beer and come sit with me," she said to Clint, and hurried away to a table. Along the way men called out "Belle," and she waved to them. Clint grabbed his beer and followed. The men in the place gave him curious looks, wondering what he had done to deserve the attentions of Madam Varnish.

By the time he reached her table, she had seated herself, leaving him a seat with his back to the wall.

"You see?" she said. "I've learned. All you famous men, you like to sit with your backs to the wall."

Clint sat down, removed his hat and looked across the table at her.

"Now, what brings you back to White Oaks after all these years?" she asked.

"Passing through," he lied. "Thought I'd see how the place had grown."

"Four thousand people, last count."

"Couldn't tell that from the street."

"Most of them are in the mines, or working at their jobs, or at home," she said. "And on their ranches. Census counts all of the people in the county."

"I see. Somehow, the town looks different, though."

"The War," she said. When she said the word, he could hear the capital W.

"The Lincoln County War?" he asked. "That was hardly a war, Belle. It only lasted five days."

"To the folks in Lincoln County," she said, "it was a war. You should know, Clint. You were here for it."

"I wasn't here for the, uh, war," he said. "I'd left by then."

"You were here for the buildup," she said. "You witnessed everything but the actual war."

"Do the people here still take it that seriously, Belle?"

"Oh yes," she said. "It will take many years for the hot feelings here to die away."

"And all because of Billy."

"Partially because of Billy," she said. "Ah, the girls here, they all loved him."

"But . . . he was a boy."

"A boy with a special talent, though."

"You mean with a gun?" Clint asked. "That's not a good talent to have, Belle—"

"No, not with a gun," she said, "with his feet."

"I don't follow," he said. "His feet?"

"That boy could dance!" Belle said, laughing. "He danced all the young girls into the ground. Tired one out and moved onto the next, till they were all plumb tuckered out."

"Don't people still dance around here?"

"Not so much since Billy was murdered."

"Murdered?" Clint asked. "That's a harsh way of putting it."

"Garrett shot him down in cold blood, Clint," she said. "Everybody knows that."

"Not everybody, Belle," Clint said. "Garrett was the law—"

"Did you ever meet him?"

"Not while I was here," he admitted, "but I did a little while back. We had some dealings—"

"He was a coward and a blowhard, and a traitor," she said. "Billy was his friend."

"I gotta tell you, Belle," Clint said, "to most folks it appeared that Billy was out of control and Garrett was doing his job. Billy had killed—"

"Five people," she said. "Five." She held up a spread hand to illustrate. "Not no twenty-one like the dime novels said. You should know about that, Clint. You ain't done all the things the dime novels say you have."

"Maybe not," Clint admitted, "but five is still a lot, and some of them were lawmen."

"Billy was railroaded—"

Clint held his hands up and said, "I'm not here to argue with you about Billy, Belle. I'm not here to argue the, uh, war, either. I just stopped in to see an old friend."

Belle leaned back and smiled.

"I'm sorry, Clint," she said. "I guess that damn war ain't over for me, either. You want some food?"

"I could eat."

She stood up and said, "And then some company, huh? Girls have come and gone since you was here, but I got some fine ones—"

"Belle, you know I don't—"

"Won't charge you for that, either," she promised. "Or the food. Everything's on the house for Clint Adams."

Clint grinned and said, "You drive a hard bargain, Madam Varnish."

THREE

The blonde's name was Ruby, and she was just as good as the free beer and free meal Belle La Mar had provided for Clint. Belle had dined with Clint, both of them consuming equal portions of beef stew before she called Ruby over to introduce her.

"Clint, this vision is Ruby," she said, as the full-breasted blonde sidled over to him and pressed a well-rounded, firm hip up against his shoulder. "Ruby, this is my friend Clint. You are to be very, very nice to him."

"My pleasure," Ruby said, looking down at Clint.

"Clint," Belle asked, "do you want a room upstairs, or will you be taking a room at the hotel?"

"The hotel, I think," Clint said, then looked at Ruby and added, "if that's all right with you?"

"It's fine with me," Ruby said.

"I have to take care of my horse," he said, "and then check in."

"Ruby will be over later, then," Belle said, "after you get . . . comfortable."

Clint stood up and found that Ruby was a rather big girl, with height to go with her full breasts and hips. Her skin was creamy and her hair shimmered. He guessed that she was about twenty-eight, if not thirty yet. Her lips were full, and she had just the hint of a double chin. She looked like she belonged in a painting hanging over most of the bars in the West.

"Until later, then," he said.

"Later." She bounced her hip off of his and licked her lower lip. As long as he wasn't paying the freight, he looked forward to licking that lower lip himself.

"Belle."

"Clint, it's good to see you."

"You, too." He executed a slight bow. "Ladies."

He put Eclipse up at the livery and checked into the hotel, and then settled into his room to wait for Ruby. Why not? A little harmless fun was in order after the ride he'd taken to get here. He certainly hadn't been "just passing through" as he'd told Belle. His presence in White Oaks had been requested, and he was there to do a job—or a favor, as it had been put to him. But also, he was there to satisfy his own curiosity. After all, it wasn't every day somebody asked you to go looking for the ghost of Billy the Kid, was it?

When the knock came on the door, Clint got off the bed and answered it with his shirt and boots off, his Levi's on and his gun in his hand.

"Who is it?"

"It's Ruby," the girl's voice said. "Madam Varnish sent me?"

Clint opened the door with his left hand and kept the right hand, holding the gun, behind his back.

"Can I come in?"

"Of course, Ruby."

As the girl went by him, Clint noticed two things. One, she smelled wonderful. Two, she *was* a big girl—bigger than he'd first thought. Not fat, but solidly built, and tall.

As he closed the door, she turned and saw the gun in his hand.

"I don't think you're going to need that," she said. She was wearing a shawl over her shoulders and let it drop. Her dress was tight, and low cut, and her cleavage was impressive, to say the least. "If you think I'm armed, you can search me."

"This was just a precaution," he said, indicating the gun in his hand, "until I knew who was at the door."

"Are you an outlaw?" she asked. "On the run?"

"Belle didn't tell you my name?"

"No," Ruby said. "She said the name wasn't important, as long as I knew that you were a special friend of hers and I was to treat you right."

"Let me just put this away." He walked to where his holster was hanging on the headboard and slid the gun home. As he turned, he saw that Ruby was coming around to his side of the bed. Her dress seemed to have slipped down from her shoulders.

"You have a nice chest," she said, touching him as she reached him. Her fingertips were cool.

"So do you," he said, looking down at her deep cleavage, "and beautiful skin." Smooth and clear, and very firm, he imagined. Well, he didn't have to imagine. Her hands were moving over his chest, so he decided to return the favor.

He gave the dress a tug on either side and that was all it needed to slide from her shoulders and fall to the floor. What he saw made him catch his breath. Her breasts were incredibly large, and yet they were firm, with hardly any sag. She had come prepared and was wearing no underwear at all. He could see the blonde hair around her pink-skinned portal, and he could smell her tangy scent already.

"I know," she said, with a pout, "I'm kind of a big girl—too big for some men."

"Not too big for me," he said. He touched both breasts, flicking her pink nipples with his thumbs, and then sliding his hands beneath them to cup their weight.

"No," he said to Ruby, "I don't think we're going to have any problem here at all."

FOUR

Clint lifted the marvelously large and heavy breasts to his mouth, kissed each in turn and sucked the nipples until they were hard in his mouth. Meanwhile, Ruby slid her hands down so she could rub him through his trousers, and her touch was having the desired effect.

"We better get this out in the open before it bursts out on its own," she said.

He didn't object when she went to her knees in front of him, undid his pants, reached in and freed his erection.

"Oh my," she said, "and you said *I* was big."

"Well," he asked, "will we have any trouble there?"

"Oh no," she breathed, "no trouble at all." And to illustrate her point she took him in his mouth, sucked him up and down a few times to get him good and wet, and then took him all the way into her mouth, accommodating the entire length of him.

"Oh, Jesus . . . ," he groaned.

"See?" she said, letting him slide free of her mouth.

"No trouble at all." She bestowed a kiss on the shiny, spongy head of his cock, and then took it between her breasts, rolling it there. Every so often she'd flick out her tongue to catch the head and he'd jump, his penis was so sensitive.

Realizing he hadn't even kissed her yet, he reached down for her and drew her to her feet. She was wearing shoes and he was in his bare feet and they almost stood nose to nose. He kissed her then, gently at first, testing her lips with his, using his tongue, but then she opened her mouth beneath his and they melted into a long, hot, deep, wet kiss that curled both their toes. Her heavy breasts were pressed tightly to his chest, and he could feel the heat of her groin against his. His erect penis was now trapped between their bodies, and he reached around to cup her firm, chunky buttocks so he could pull her even more tightly to him. She moaned into his mouth and reached around to dig her nails into his buttocks, as well.

She broke the kiss then, breathless, and began to kiss his chest, his nipples, down lower to his belly and lower still until she had him in her mouth again. She sucked him avidly, drawing him up onto his toes. He tried to disengage from her, tried to get away before it was too late. But she was having none of it. With one hand she fondled his testicles, and with the other she drew a nail along the underside of his dick. Finally, she reached around again to grab his ass cheeks and hold on tightly to him as he exploded into her mouth. She was extraordinarily good at this, he realized, as she accommodated every drop he had to offer without any difficulty.

"Jesus," he said, when she finally released him from her mouth, "I think you drained me."

"Oh no," she said, taking his semi-erect dick into her hand, "you're more man than that. I can tell."

She leaned forward and began to lick and suck him

again, and before long they both had proof that she was right.

It had the makings of a long night.

Long, but extremely pleasurable. He'd been with women of all sizes and shapes in his life—fat, skinny, tall, short—but this woman was equal and perfect parts of everything. Her body was so firm, but so well-rounded, it seemed to defy gravity. Her thighs were large, but proportioned to her so that they appeared perfect. There was extra flesh on her, around her belly and her hips, but he would have missed it now if it suddenly wasn't there. And her scent—well, her skin had its own, and her hair, and her vagina, and when you mixed them altogether you came away with a perfume that was unique to her.

Later that evening he laid her on her belly so he could roam her body with his hands and his tongue. There seemed to be acres of pale blond girl in front of him, and he wanted to touch it all. He kissed her back, licked the cleft between her ass cheeks, slid his hand beneath her so he could probe her from behind. She lifted her belly off the bed to give him more access and became immediately wet when he touched her. He'd never before known a woman who could get so wet so quickly, and it soaked into the sheets beneath them. The room became filled with the scent of their lovemaking. He fingered her as he kissed her buttocks and she became impatient. She turned over, grabbed for his head and pulled it to her. He used his tongue to explore her pubic bush and push past it so he could lick and taste her. She groaned as his tongue played over her, pushed aside the folds of her vagina so he could enter her, then backed up again to find her rigid clit as taut as a guitar string, waiting for his tongue to give her sweet release. He flicked at it, sucked it, rolled it, and suddenly her belly trembled, her legs quivered, her calf muscles stood out as she lifted her majestic butt off the bed and then exploded into a frenzy of movement. He could feel her gushing, and he lapped it up like it was honey, while at the same time using his arms to keep her down, and his hands to hold onto her and keep her from actually tossing him off the bed.

And before the last tremors of her orgasm could fade away, he got to his knees, spread her legs and speared her, bringing a gasp from her lips and causing her eyes to open wide. He rode her that way, then taking hold of her ankles so he could spread her even wider, he pounded away at her until he achieved his own release. He groaned out loud as she once again drained him, and it seemed that she was sucking him dry as much this time as she had last time, with her mouth. She had even more talent than he'd thought—and there was more to come.

Later he took her from behind, she on her hands and knees, that wondrous butt slamming back against him as he drove forward into her. The entire bed shook and occasionally leaped off the floor, and he wondered why no one was coming to knock at the door and see what was going on. Surely they could be heard not only from the hotel, but from the street as well . . .

And still later she rode him, sitting astride him with his cock buried deep inside of her. She lifted up and came down on him with such force that he swore this was the deepest he had ever been inside a woman.

"God," she gasped at one point, "I think I can feel you right here," pointing to a spot between her breasts . . .

Finally, Ruby seemed to have had enough and fell into a deep sleep. Clint thought he should have been exhausted, trying to keep up with this incredibly healthy young woman, but instead he was wide awake.

He quit the bed without waking her and walked to the window. As he stared down at the empty main street of White Oaks his thoughts drifted back to the first time he'd come to Lincoln County.

PART ONE

FIVE

LINCOLN COUNTY, FEBRUARY 1878

When Clint had first come to Lincoln County, New Mexico, it had been at the behest of John Chisum. He'd known Chisum when the cattleman had a spread in West Texas. Now the man had a ranch three miles south of Roswell, and he'd sent a message asking Clint to come and see him. They were never good friends, but Clint knew Chisum, and knew the man would rather cut off his arm than ask for help.

Clint rode Duke from Labyrinth, Texas, to Roswell and presented himself to John Chisum at his ranch. It was a huge spread, he knew that going in. Some said Chisum has eighty thousand head of cattle. But Clint was still shocked at the sheer size of the place, and the opulence with which it was furnished.

He was met by Chisum's foreman in front of the house. The man had someone walk Duke to the barn and then the foreman, a man named Johnny Boggs, showed Clint to Chisum's office.

"Clint, good of you to come." Chisum rose from behind his desk. He was a big man in his late thirties. He'd made his fortune early, and it continued to grow as he got older.

"You've met Sweet Johnny, I see."

"Sweet Johnny?" Clint asked.

"Not a name I cultivate," Boggs said, "but then we don't pick what people call us, do we?"

Clint Adams—The Gunsmith—knew that very well.

"Sweet Johnny Boggs," the man said, and stuck out his hand. Boggs was about forty, with a wild growth of beard and a ready smile.

"Clint Adams." The two shook hands.

"Johnny, you can stay while I talk to Clint," Chisum said, reclaiming the chair behind his desk.

"If it's all the same to you, Boss," Boggs said, "I know what you're gonna talk about, and I got some work to do."

"Suit yourself."

Boggs looked at Clint and said, "See you around."

"Sure."

Boggs left and Clint turned to face Chisum.

"Have a seat, Clint," the rancher said. "Drink?"

"Maybe later, John," Clint said. "Right now I'm curious about what it would take for you to send me a distress call."

"Distress," Chisum said, shaking his head. "I guess that's as good a word as any for it."

Clint remained silent and waited for Chisum to elaborate.

"How much do you know about Lincoln County?"

"Nothing."

"Well, I guess that's good," Chisum said. "At least you won't have taken sides."

"How many sides are there?"

"Two," Chisum said. "There's the Murphy side. Actually, it's the Murphy and Dolan side. They have long been the only faction in the county running a huge general store called the House, buying cattle, having a monopoly on government contracts to supply cattle and horses until Tunstall and McSween decided to compete."

"None of those names means anything to me," Clint said. "Which side are you backing?"

"John Tunstall and Alex McSween," Chisum said.

"Why?"

"McSween has been my lawyer for some time," Chisum said. "Tunstall is a young Englishman come here to make his way. They felt there was a need in Lincoln for another general store, and for a bank, which we've never had before. So they set them up, with my backing. They also decided to go after the government contracts, thereby competing with Lawrence Murphy, who didn't take kindly to it."

"And what has the result been?"

"Hard feelings," Chisum said. "Hatred, actually, and, I fear, soon there will be violence, killing."

"Why?"

"Murphy and Dolan have gunmen working for them," Chisum said. "They also have the local law, Sheriff Brady, in their pocket. For this reason Tunstall has decided to gather together some Regulators."

"More hired guns," Clint said. Ranchers had collected Regulators before, and the outcome was usually a bloodbath. "Can you talk him out of it?"

"I don't think so," Chisum said. "That's why I called for you."

"What can I do?"

"Maybe you can put a lid on this," Chisum said. "You've had experience, after all—probably more than any of the parties involved, including me."

"How do you suggest I do this?"

"Talk to everyone concerned," Chisum said. "You have a reputation. They'll listen to you."

"You think so?"

"I hope so," Chisum answered. "I want this stopped before it gets out of hand, Clint. I'll pay you whatever you want."

"What about federal intervention?"

"I'm trying to avoid that, for now," Chisum replied. "Maybe your presence will do something."

Clint doubted it, but it was an interesting proposition, and not only for the offer of payment of any amount.

"Will you do it?" Chisum asked. "Will you try?"

"John . . . I can only try, okay?' Clint said. "I can't promise anything."

"I'm just trying to head off a war, Clint," Chisum said. "All I want is your help to do that."

Clint stood up, and Chisum stood and put out his hand.

"I'll try."

SIX

Clint declined Chisum's offer to stay on his ranch. He had to at least appear impartial if he was going to talk with all the parties involved, so he decided to stay in a hotel in Lincoln.

Clint rode into Lincoln because that's where Murphy's store—called the "House" or just the "Big Store"—was. Down the street from the store was the Wortley Hotel, and that's where Clint went to register. The store run by Tunstall and McSween was also nearby. Clint wondered why they had not built their store farther away, but perhaps they had built it close by in the spirit of competition—a spirit which Lawrence Murphy apparently did not appreciate.

After registering at the hotel, Clint took Duke to a nearby livery stable and left him in the hands of the liveryman.

"Beautiful animal," the man said, admiring the huge gelding.

"Just be careful of him," Clint said. "He likes fingers."

The liveryman held up one hand, showing Clint that he was already missing a finger and a half.

"Been around horses all my life, mister," he said, which Clint assumed to mean over sixty years. "A finger or two ain't too much to ask for taking care of an animal like this."

"Well, I warned you," Clint said.

"Hey," the man said, as Clint started to leave, "don't I know you?"

"Do you?" Clint asked, and continued on.

Clint decided to take a couple of days to get the lay of the land in Lincoln—not only the town, but the county. He drank in the saloon, ate in local restaurants in Lincoln, White Oaks and nearby Carrizozo, as well as Fort Sumner. He learned that folks were pretty much split down the middle when it came to taking sides. It seemed like most of the ranchers in the area sided with Murphy, while the townspeople took Tunstall's side. He also found out that Murphy had sold most of his interest in the Big Store to John Riley and J. J. Dolan.

Most of the ranchers had smaller spreads than Chisum, and resented him for it. They also objected to his use of most of the public grazing land for his eighty thousand head. Clint felt they had aligned themselves with the men who owned the Big Store not so much out of liking for them but for the possibility that Murphy-Dolan-Riley might have been able to rid the area of the larger, more successful cattleman.

He also learned that Tunstall had his own spread, the Flying H Ranch. Apparently, he simply retained the name the ranch had when he bought it. He was also still hiring men Clint assumed would become part of the "Regulators" Chisum had spoken of.

After a few days Clint decided on the order in which he would speak to the principals. He thought he'd talk to

Murphy or Dolan or Riley first, then speak with Tunstall and McSween. But first he decided to go and see Sheriff William Brady.

Brady's office was in Carrizozo, but he could have been anywhere in the county—Lincoln, or even White Oaks—when Clint went looking for him. Luckily, he found the man right in his office at the time.

William Brady was a portly, almost fat man who carried neither his weight nor his badge with very much authority. When Clint walked in he was sitting at his desk, eating his lunch with much gusto and very little regard for where the food might go other than his mouth. Both his desk and the floor beneath it were littered with remnants of not only this meal, but meals gone by, as well.

"Sheriff Brady?"

"I'm havin' my lunch now."

"But you are Sheriff Brady?"

"That's right," Brady said. He still had not look up from his sandwich.

"The Sheriff Brady who has thrown in with the owners of the Big Store?" Clint asked, deciding to shake the man up if he could. "Murphy, Dolan and Riley?"

That caught the lawman's attention and he finally looked up at Clint, although that did not keep him from taking another large bite from his sandwich.

"Who are you?" Brady asked. "What right you got comin' in here and talkin' to me that way? I oughta toss your ass in jail."

"I don't think I've broken any law in your town yet," Clint said, "and I'm not accusing you of anything. I'm just repeating some gossip I've been hearing around town."

"Yeah, well, don't believe everything you hear, stranger. And you still ain't told me your name."

"You're right, I haven't," Clint said. He stepped closer

to the badge. He did not often speak his name hoping for a certain effect, but he did so now.

"My name is Clint Adams."

The sheriff had been in the act of bringing the sandwich to his mouth yet again, but the name arrested the motion. He laid the sandwich down on the desk and looked at Clint much more closely, this time.

"The, uh, Gunsmith Clint Adams?"

"That's right, Sheriff," Clint said. "That's what some people have been known to call me."

SEVEN

Brady pushed his chair back, but seemed unsure about what to do next—remain seated or stand up.

"Well, what—I mean, who—why are you in, uh, Carrizozo?"

"Actually," Clint said, "I'm in Lincoln, but I just thought I'd come over and let you know I was in the county."

"Uh, well, I appreciate that . . . I guess. Any idea how long you'll be stayin'?"

"I'm not sure," Clint said, "but I thought I'd check in with you on some talk I've been hearing."

"Uh, w-what kind of talk?"

"Well, I'm hearing lots of names to see about, names I'm not familiar with, like Murphy and Dolan, like Tunstall and McSween and Chisum—well, I know John Chisum."

"You do?" Brady asked. "Uh, you're . . . friends?"

"Well, I wouldn't say that," Clint replied. "I mean I

know the man. He's a pretty famous cattleman, after all."

"Uh, yeah, he is."

"Is he taking sides in this thing?" Clint asked, acting ignorant of the facts.

"Uh, there's no—I don't know what—why are you interested in this?" Brady finally asked, after stammering.

"Hey, I just rode into the county, you know, passing through, and I'm hearing all kinds of talk. Seems to me the county is divided pretty evenly between the two factions."

"Factions?"

"Both sides."

"Oh, well . . . I'm the law here, uh, Mr. Adams, I really can't take sides."

"Well, that's an admirable position to take, Sheriff," Clint said. "The talk I've been hearing has you on the side of the Big Store."

"That's not true!" Brady snapped. "Uh, I'm, uh, I can't really—I got work to do."

"What about your lunch?"

Brady grabbed his hat and looked mournfully down at what was left of his lunch.

"I don't have time to finish," Brady said. "I gotta go and do rounds.

"Well, I won't keep you, then," Clint said. "I just wanted to let you know I was . . . around."

"Well, I appreciate it, uh, Mr. Adams."

Clint walked out the door with Brady, and the two men parted company outside. The lawman walked away, nervously looking back over his shoulder at Clint, who stood his ground, not wanting to make it any easier on the man. Once the stout lawman was out of sight, Clint stepped down off the boardwalk and mounted Eclipse.

Meeting with the sheriff had established only that he was not much of a lawman. The ride to Carrizozo, however, had taken Clint within a relatively easy ride of White Oaks. He'd heard a lot about White Oaks since both gold and coal were discovered in the mountains, and since it was part of Lincoln County he decided to take a ride there and see if he could learn anything else from the citizens there.

As he rode down the main street, he recognized the feel of a boomtown: the hustle and bustle of people, the ruts in the street from the constant traffic, and the requisite gambling halls and saloons and cathouses that lined the streets. Gamblers, whores and out-and-out thieves waited to take the money from the miners soon after the miners took it out of the ground. And in the case of the gamblers and whores, the miners were only too glad to part with it. After all, what was money for if not to play cards and buy women?

Clint dismounted in front of one of the smaller saloons, called simply the White Oaks Saloon. He went inside, had a beer and listened to the talk going on around him. It was noisy as hell but he was able to hear snatches of different conversations. Most of the talk was of gold and women, but he heard the occasional opinions offered on which faction was going to come out on top, the Murphy-Dolan-Riley side, or the Tunstall-McSween side. Even less frequently he heard the latter described as the Tunstall-McSween-Chisum side, but for the most part Chisum's name was not mentioned.

Clint hit several of the saloons and gambling houses along White Oaks's main street, until he came to the one called Little Casino. As he entered he saw that it had everything, from beer and booze to gaming to girls. It appeared to be a combination gambling hall and whore-house, and it was doing a bang-up business.

"Can I help you, stranger?"

Clint turned and saw a woman in her early forties, with black hair and a solid body that threatened to burst the seams of her low-cut blue dress. She wasn't fat—not yet, anyway—just solid.

"My name is Belle La Mar," the woman said. "Most folks around here call me Madam Varnish."

"Well, Belle," Clint said, "my name's Clint Adams and I guess I'll just start with a beer."

"That's a good start, honey," she said. "We got the best beer in town at Little Casino, but it's only a start. We also got the best games, and the best girls. Just take a look at Starla and Stella, there."

At that moment two girls in their twenties walked by and gave Clint the eye. He didn't know which was Starla and which was Stella but one was blond and the other was a young black girl. Both were stunning. The black girl was tall and slender, and the other one was short and full-bodied, but both were beautiful.

"Well," Clint said to Madam Varnish, "from what I've seen so far, you don't lie."

"Honey," Belle said, taking his arm and leading him through the crowd to the bar, "I never lie."

EIGHT

Clint had an ice cold beer and watched the action in the place escalate as the hour got later. Finally, he decided that sitting in on a poker game might make him privy to information he might not otherwise hear.

"Sure," Bell La Mar said, "I can get you into a game. The question is, do you want the other players to know who you are?"

"Well," he said, "obviously you know, but why should they? As far as they're concerned I'm just another poker player, right?"

"Yeah, but we know you're a famous one," she said, "but that's your choice. I'll take you to a table and introduce you as just another poker player."

"I'd appreciate it."

She squinted and asked, "What are you after, Mr. Adams?"

"Right now," he said, "I'm just after some poker."

"Follow me."

She took him to a table with five players and one empty seat. Actually, there were four players, because the fifth seat was taken up by a house dealer.

"This gent would like to play some cards, boys," she said, by way of introduction. "Any objections?"

"Grab the empty seat there, friend," one man said. "The more the merrier."

"The more money, he means," a second player said, sourly.

Clint looked at the stack of chips in front of the first man and realized he was doing most of the winning. Clint bought some chips and sat back to wait for the deal. The game was draw poker rather than dealer's choice, with the house dealer doling out the cards each hand. The dealer was a stone-faced man who went about his business quietly. Soon, Clint learned that most of the players also roiled in silence, which was the way he usually liked his game. This time, however, he had hoped to pick up more information about the conflict that was going on in Lincoln County. All he found out was that the second man who had spoken was a bad loser who grumbled loud enough for everyone to hear.

Giving up on the game as a source of information, he decided to simply look for a little entertainment—and he got it. While three of the players were bad—with the grumbling loser bordering on inept—the man doing all the winning was an excellent player who immediately recognized the same trait in Clint. After a particular hand that Clint took, the man looked across the table at him and gave him a nod of respect. Clint returned the favor a hand later. It was at this point that Clint recognized the man. It was a recently shorn and cleaned up Johnny Boggs, John Chisum's foreman. Neither of them let on that they had ever met before. They played across from each for two hours and then Clint decided he'd had enough entertainment for one night. He left the table a winner, but Boggs had pretty much played even for the two hours and was still well ahead.

"Cashing out," Clint said to the dealer.

"So am I," Boggs said.

"What?" the big loser said. "Uh-uh, no, you're not cashin' out."

Clint looked at the man, but he was talking to Boggs, not to him.

"Excuse me?" Boggs asked.

"You got most of my money, friend," the man said. "I want a chance to win it back."

"You've had hours to lose it," Boggs said. "How long do you think you'll need to win it back?"

"Don't make no never mind," the man said. "You ain't leavin' until I do."

Boggs leaned forward in his chair and fixed the man with a hard look.

"How about I just give it back to you?"

"What?"

"You tell me how much you're down and I'll give it back. How's that?"

The other man looked around the table. He was being made to look silly now, and didn't like it.

"Nobody gives money back," he said.

"That's right," Boggs said. "You got about as much chance of winning the money back as you do of me givin' it back." He looked at the dealer. "Cash me out."

Clint waited for the sound of the chair scraping the floor as the loser pushed his chair back to give himself access to his gun. He leaned over and quickly clamped his hand down on the other man's gun hand, pinning his gun in his holster.

"No guns," he said.

"Are you crazy?" the man said, glaring at him. "This ain't your business."

"I've taken more of your money than he has over the

past two hours," Clint said. "Why aren't you complaining about me cashing out?"

This confused the man, but before he could recover, two men appeared behind him, standing on either side of him, and behind them was Madam Varnish.

"Do we have a problem here?" she asked.

The dealer looked at her. "This gentleman does not want these gentlemen to cash out of the game."

"Why not?" she asked.

The dealer shrugged. "Apparently, he feels they're leaving with his money."

"He was complaining about me," Boggs said. "This fella here simply stopped him from making a big mistake."

Madam Varnish saw Clint's hand pinning the loser's gun in his holster.

"Boys," she said, "show Mr. Bowdre out."

"Belle—"

"Charlie," she said, "I've told you and told you no gunplay in my place, haven't I?"

"Belle—"

"Take him out, boys."

One of the bouncers quickly removed Charlie Bowdre's gun from his holster, while the other lifted him from his seat by one arm. Once they had him standing, they each grabbed an arm and walked him to the door and outside.

"Gentlemen," Belle said to Clint and Boggs, "my apologies. Once you're cashed out, please go to the bar for a drink on the house."

"Thank you, Belle," Boggs said.

"Yes, thank you," Clint echoed.

She looked at the dealer and said, "Continue the game."

"Not enough players," the man said.

"Then close the table and take a break."

"Yes, ma'am."

Clint and Boggs both cashed out, and Clint asked,

"Would you like to have that free drink together, Mr. Boggs?"

"Why not?" Boggs agreed, and the two went to the bar together.

NINE

Clint and Sweet Johnny Boggs reached the bar and each ordered a beer.

"It was smart not to let on that we knew each other," Clint said.

"We don't, really," Boggs said, "so it wasn't really much of a stretch, was it?"

"You're not from the West, are you?"

"It shows?" Boggs asked. "No, I came here from the East after college. That was about fifteen years ago. I started cowpunching and worked my way up to ramrod."

"Cowpunching wasn't what you went to college for, was it?" Clint asked.

"No," Boggs said, "I went to college for my family. The week after I graduated, my father died. He got to see me graduate and it made him very happy. I left the day after his funeral, came out here and made myself very happy."

"Where'd you learn to play cards?"

"Out here," he said. "Never played back east, but then I learned a lot of things out here I never even heard of back east. You?"

"I came from the East also," Clint said, "but that was a long time ago." And that was all he was willing to say on the matter.

They finished their beers and Clint said, "I'll buy one."

"Suits me."

When they were refilled, he asked, "Who was the loser?"

"Charlie Bowdre," Boggs said. "One of Tunstall's men."

"Seems hotheaded."

"He's hiring gunhands, and a lot of them are young, like Charlie," Boggs said. "Young and hotheaded."

"That's not a good combination," Clint said, "guns and hotheads."

"That's why I only hire experienced men on Chisum's ranch."

"I'll bet John appreciates that."

"He pays me well for what I do," Boggs said, "as long as I do it well."

"How will Bowdre take being . . . helped out of here tonight?"

"Wasn't the first time, won't be the last," Boggs said. "Charlie shouldn't play poker. He's just bad at it. The sooner he learns that the better."

"Bad poker players never believe they're bad," Clint observed. "And they never learn. He's going to get himself killed at a poker table one day, with that attitude."

"That's his business." Boggs finished his beer and set the mug down. "I'll buy one and then I've got to get back."

After they were refilled again, Clint asked, "What's your take on this whole business, Johnny?"

"This whole county is set to explode, Clint," Boggs

said. "The Big Store, that's the powderkeg, and Tunstall is the fuse."

"And the match?"

Boggs looked at Clint for a moment, then said, "The match might very well be a young fella named William Bonney."

Boggs told Clint about a youngster who was called Billy the Kid.

"Fast with his mouth, good with a gun," Boggs said, "too young to be doing the things he's been doing."

"Like what?"

"Well," Boggs said, "story goes Billy and his mother came west from New York. When they reached Oklahoma his ma was raped by two men. Billy ended up here, taught himself to use a gun, and then—supposedly—left here, tracked those men down and killed them, and then came back."

"Why here?"

"You know anything about Tunstall?"

"No."

"He's twenty-three years old."

"I would have thought he'd be older."

"He and Billy get along," Boggs said, "and Billy has a lot of friends here. Remember I talked about hotheads? Well, Billy's the hottest. You mark my words, Billy's going to do something to touch this whole thing off."

"Have you told Chisum what you think?"

"Mr. Chisum makes his own decisions," Boggs said. "He listens to what I have to say when it comes to the ranch, but not with his other business. Him investing in Tunstall's store and bank"—Boggs took a moment to shake his head—"I never thought that was a good idea, but it wasn't my place to say."

"Maybe he would have appreciated your counsel."

"Maybe," Boggs said, finishing off his beer. "I've got

to get back. It was interesting playing poker with you. Maybe we can do it again."

"I hope so."

"This is where I play," Boggs said. "The deal here is as honest as you're going to get."

"I'll remember that."

"And the women are clean," Boggs said. "Belle sees to that."

"I'll remember that, too."

The two men shook hands and Johnny Boggs left the Little Casino. Just for a moment Clint wondered if he should have gone with him, in case Charlie Bowdre was waiting outside, but then he decided not. Boggs seemed like a man who could take care of himself. He listened for the sound of gunshots, but none came, and pretty soon he turned and asked the bartender for another beer.

TEN

"Well," Belle La Mar said, coming up next to him, "you've had some excitement, some of my beer and some poker. You ready to try one of my girls?"

He turned to her, beer mug in hand, and his eyes were drawn to her firm cleavage.

"Belle," he said, "I'd love to try one of your beautiful girls, but the fact of the matter is I never pay for a woman."

"Never?"

"Never have, never will."

Belle eyed him critically, then said, "Well, it's my guess you've never had to."

He laughed and said, "I do okay."

"You're a pretty good poker player, too, by all accounts."

She'd either watched him, or talked to her dealer, or both.

"I do okay there, too."

42

"How long will you be stayin' in town?"

"I've got a hotel room in Lincoln waiting for me."

"Too bad," she said, "you and me, maybe we could have arranged somethin'."

He didn't know if she meant her, or one of her girls, but the offer would have been interesting either way.

"Maybe another time, Belle."

"You come back in here, Clint Adams," she said, "maybe I can fix you up."

"I'll keep that offer in mind, Belle."

As she started to turn away he said, "Belle?"

"Change your mind already?"

"No, I just wanted to ask you something. I've been hearing rumors around Lincoln that there's trouble brewing."

"You talkin' about Dolan and Tunstall? Sure, what else could you be talkin' about? Yeah, it's brewin'."

"Can you tell me what it's about?"

"It's about men bein' men," she said, "or rather, boys bein' boys, and bein' stupid. You don't want to get involved in this, Clint . . . or do you? You ain't here to hire on to one side or the other, are you?"

"Why would you ask that?"

"Just thought you might be tryin' to figure out which side's gonna be the winnin' one."

"No," he said, "I don't know Dolan or Tunstall. I've just been hearing talk and wanted to see what your take was on it."

"Well, you were playin' poker with two fellas who may have somethin' to do with the outcome."

"Was I?"

"Charlie Bowdre, he rides with Billy for Tunstall," she said, "and Sweet Johnny, he rides for Chisum, and Chisum is backin' Tunstall."

He found it curious that she referred to Bonney simply

as "Billy." Did everyone in Lincoln know the boy? he wondered.

"Boggs?"

"He's Chisum's foreman."

"Why is he called Sweet Johnny?"

She grinned and said, "Obviously you've never seen him smile."

"I have the feeling he rarely smiles at the poker table," Clint observed.

"Well, when he does it's a sight to behold," she said. "Sweetest smile you'd ever wanna see."

"That's so?"

"My girls like it, that's for sure," she said. "Anything else I can help you with?"

"No," he said, "I think I'll just head back to my lonely hotel room in Lincoln."

"If it is lonely," she said, "it's your own damn fault."

As she turned and walked, he muttered, "Most things are," and headed for the door.

ELEVEN

During the ride back to Lincoln in the dark—a bad decision, but too late to do anything about it now—Clint considered the things he had learned. Apparently, this Billy the Kid figured to be a catalyst in the fracas that was coming. He wondered how much Chisum knew about the boy. Since he was working for Tunstall—one of his Regulators, no doubt—the rancher probably knew plenty, but maybe he was leaving it to Clint to learn things on his own.

So he knew two of the Regulators' names—Charlie Bowdre and William Bonney. If they worked for Tunstall, did that mean they also worked for McSween? Or did Tunstall keep his ranch separate from his store? Certainly McSween must have had his own home.

And what about Murphy? How involved was he anymore? Or were Dolan and Riley the main players on that side now? Tomorrow he'd stop into the Big Store and talk with one of them, get the lay of the land there.

Although he was unfamiliar with the country here, he believed he was heading directly for Lincoln. He had Duke moving at an easy gait, not wanting to take a chance on the big gelding stepping into a chuckhole in the dark. Eventually, however, he became aware that someone was following him. He didn't just think someone was there, he knew it, because they were making no attempt to hide the fact. He wondered if it was Charlie Bowdre, riding after him to take some sort of revenge. Or maybe Johnny Boggs. He decided to find out who it was before they reached Lincoln. He reined Duke in when they came to a clump of trees, and guided the gelding behind them. There was a full moon, so he knew he'd be able to see who the rider was once they caught up to him.

After a few moments of waiting, he could hear the approaching horse's hooves. Whoever the rider was, they were moving faster than he had been, obviously trying to catch up. He listened as horse and rider approached, timed it right, and then rode out to intercept them. The rider reined their horse in abruptly, causing the animal to rear, then slid from the back of the horse and landed on the ground on their butt. The horse continued on, but at a slower pace. It would not be difficult to catch.

Clint dismounted and approached the fallen rider.

"Okay, let's hear why you're following me." He reached down, grabbed the rider by the shirt and yanked him to his feet, only to find that he was holding onto a girl, not a man.

"What the—" he said, releasing her.

"Jesus," she said. She staggered back a few steps, then stopped and started rubbing her butt. "What'd you wanna do, kill me?"

"I didn't know—" he said. "I mean, I thought you were following me—"

"I was," she said. "At least, I was trying to catch up to you."

"But . . . why?"

"Belle sent me," she said. "She told me you needed some company tonight."

"Belle La Mar sent you after me?"

"That's right."

"On horseback, at night?"

"I'm a good rider," she said. "I don't normally get thrown, but you scared me and my horse half to death."

"I'm sorry," he said. "I thought you were someone else."

"Well, I'm not," she said. "I'm me, or what's left of me."

"I'm really sorry," he said. "Are you hurt? Can I do anything for you?"

"Well, you can find my horse," she said, "and then I guess you can tell me if you do or don't want some company tonight."

"I'll find your horse," he said, "but I explained to Belle that I don't pay—"

"I know, I know," the woman said, "you're some special case, you don't pay for women. She knows that. I'm supposed to tell you that I'm on the house."

"On the house? But why?"

"I don't know. Belle didn't tell me why. She just told me to catch up to you. She's my boss. I do what she pays me to do."

"I don't understand—look, let me get your horse. I don't know how far we are from Lincoln—"

"It's just over the next ridge," she said. "We could walk, but I'd prefer to ride."

"Of course."

"And I'd prefer not to have to ride back to White Oaks tonight."

"I understand," he said. "Let me just get your horse and then we can . . . What's your name?"

"Fiona."

"Pretty name."

"Thanks."

In the light of the full moon he could see that she was extremely pretty, like the others he had seen. She had long dark hair and white, luminous skin.

"Uh, my horse?"

"Oh, right." He realized he'd been staring. "I'll be right back."

He mounted Duke, rode ahead twenty or thirty yards and found the horse standing calmly. He gathered up the reigns and led the animal back to its rider.

"Thanks."

"Do you need help mounting?" he asked, preparing to dismount himself.

"No," she said, "I told you, I'm an accomplished rider."

"Oh, right." That would explain why Belle felt she could send the woman out on horseback at night.

"Shall I lead the way?" she asked. "I mean, since I know where we're going?"

"By all means," he said. "Take the lead."

"My butt is gonna be sore in the morning," she muttered, "and not for the usual reasons."

TWELVE

When they reached Lincoln they went directly to the livery stable. They had to wake the liveryman in order for him to take their horses inside.

"You can stay the night here and go back to White Oaks in the morning," Clint told Fiona as they walked away from the stable.

"I thought that was the idea."

"No," he said, "I mean you can get your own room."

"Why would I want to do that?" she asked. "Don't you want me?"

"It's not that—"

"Why don't we go to your room first?" she said. "You can see what you're turning down before you turn it down."

"Fiona—"

"Come on," she said. "Don't get me into trouble with Belle. After all, I've ridden all this way, and I fell on my ass—it was your fault, don't forget. You owe me."

"All right," he said. "I do owe you, for making your horse dump you."

They went into the Wortley and he took her to his room. The hotel was an unusual one, because each of the rooms had its own door on the outside of the building. You only had to go inside to register, or to eat in the restaurant or drink in the bar. Also, the entire hotel only had seven rooms, which appealed to Clint. Less noise.

Once in the room they were able to get a better look at each other. She was wearing riding clothes, jeans and a man's shirt. No skirt and riding sidesaddle for this gal. He liked that.

"Well?" she asked. "What do you think? I'm not exactly dressed to impress but—"

"You look great," he said, and she did. Her hair was not only dark, but very long, and wavy. Her skin was pale, and her lips had a naturally rosy color to them. Her eyes were large and seemed dark, even black. "Beautiful."

"All of Belle's girls are beautiful," she said. "She insists on it."

"Then how do men pick which one they want?"

"Well," she said, "we're all beautiful, but in different ways. There are blondes, redheads, Stella is even black. She has the most beautiful dark skin . . ."

"Your skin is lovely," he said. "So pale, and smooth."

She appeared to be in her mid to late twenties, as had the other girls he'd seen. "Girls" was probably the wrong word. Belle La Mar seemed to prefer to employ women.

"Then I can stay?" she asked. "You like what you see?"

"I like you very much," he said, "but you don't have to stay—"

"I don't have money for my own room."

"I'll get you a room."

"Where? Here? They only have seven, and there probably ain't one available."

"We can go across the street—"

"I'd rather just stay inside," she said, moving closer to him. "If you don't mind."

The closer she got, the less he minded.

He peeled her clothes from her, revealing a long, lean body with slim hips and small breasts. Her dark skin and dark pubic patch went with her dark eyes and dark hair to create quite a picture.

"My god," he said, "you're stunning."

"Why, thank you, sir. Now you."

He stood still while she undressed him, and by the time she had him naked his penis was standing at full attention.

"Well," she said, "you're kinda stunning yourself, aren't you?"

"Nice of you to say."

She stepped close to him then, pressing against him and lifting her face to be kissed. Her lips were thin, her mouth wide and avid. It was obvious she enjoyed kissing for she used everything—lips, teeth, tongue, her entire face. She moaned deep in her throat as his own tongue pressed into her mouth.

Still in a clinch they moved to the bed and fell on it. Clint used his superior strength and weight to turn over and put Fiona on the bottom, and then proceeded to familiarize himself with her body. By the time he was done, she was pleading with him to fuck her, so he moved up and slid his penis smoothly into her wetness.

She wrapped legs, which were slender but deceptively strong, around his waist. He slipped his hands beneath her and took hold of her neat little bottom. They writhed together on the bed, grinding and lunging at one another until they were covered with sweat, and then suddenly they were there, so close to the edge, and then over it, first one and then the other soon after . . .

•   •   •

Later he said, "That Madam Varnish is sure generous with her girls."

Fiona had her head on his shoulder and her long legs entangled with him. "You think so? Generous to you maybe, but not to her girls. You know what?"

"What?"

"I think she's just trying to get you to come back and pay later."

"By sending me her best girl?"

"Exactly."

"Well, sweetie," he said, "as good as you are—and you are marvelous—I'm afraid I can't break a lifetime rule even for you."

"I don't care," she said, snuggling closer to him. "This night's not even done, so let's not talk about the future."

In moments she was asleep, snoring just lightly. Clint wondered about the generosity of Madam Varnish. What had he done to deserve it? Nothing that he knew of. That led to only one other question.

What was she going to expect him to do?

INTERLUDE

THIRTEEN

White Oaks, Lincoln County, Back to the Present

Ruby left in the early morning hours, after testing and possibly taxing Clint to the fullest. After she left, he fell right to sleep, bathed in the warmth and scent she left behind on the sheets. Madam Varnish was still generous with her girls, and maybe this time simply out of the goodness of her heart—unlike last time.

The next morning Clint went downstairs and had breakfast at a nearby café. He and Ruby had talked only briefly during the night, preferring to do other things with their energy. He hadn't collected very much information about what he'd come to find out. The Lincoln County law had its office in Lincoln now, so it seemed that would be his next stop. He'd take a ride over there after breakfast, but retain his room here in White Oaks. He'd be closer to Ruby that way. The woman had made a very good impression on him, and he wanted to see her again. While she was physically very different from Fiona—Madam Varnish's first "gift" years ago—the two women had something else in common—their seemingly endless energy, and their boundless passion.

Clint saddled Eclipse himself and set out from White Oaks to Lincoln. The sheriff's office in Lincoln was in the same building Billy the Kid had escaped from in 1881 after killing two lawmen. Clint tied Eclipse to a hitching post in front and entered the building. The sheriff's office was on the second floor. He went upstairs, found the door and knocked.

"Come!"

He didn't know who the sheriff of Lincoln County was so he was surprised when he entered and found a young man wearing the sheriff's badge. He checked again and confirmed that he was right, it was not a deputy's badge, but the sheriff's.

"Can I help you?" the man asked. He couldn't have been thirty yet. However he got the job, Clint couldn't believe that he was long for it.

"Are you the sheriff?" Clint asked. He couldn't help himself.

"That's right," the man said. He had been seated and now stood up. He was wearing a black vest over a white shirt and a pair of black trousers. Maybe he thought wearing black would make him look older, or more authoritative.

Or maybe Clint just wasn't being fair to the man—the young man.

"Sheriff Dave Eidson." The lawman did not offer to shake hands. "And you are?"

"My name is Clint Adams," Clint said, introducing himself. "I'm passing through—"

"The Gunsmith?" the sheriff said, cutting him off.

"That's right."

"I hope you don't think I'm overly impressed."

That stopped Clint cold. He wasn't used to this kind of attitude from young men—especially lawmen.

"I beg your pardon?"

"Old-timers like you," the sheriff said, "you're always coming in here announcing who you are and waiting for me to be impressed."

"Old-timers?"

"With your big reps," Eidson said.

"Have you given this attitude to somebody before me?" Clint asked.

"Well . . . no . . ."

"I didn't think so."

"What do you mean?"

"If you talked to Bat Masterson or Wyatt Earp like this, you wouldn't stay on your feet for very long—or in this job."

"Are you threatening me?" The young man puffed up his chest. He was a big young man, well over six feet and deep chested. He was wearing a new looking Colt on his hip, with a pearl handle. "I'm the law here, you know."

"Yeah? How did that happen?"

"I was elected."

"Anybody run against you?"

"Now listen, Adams—"

"Okay," Clint said, holding up his hands in an effort to placate the sheriff. "Wait a minute. We got off on the wrong foot here."

"We sure did," Eidson said. "I suggest you get back on your horse and ride out."

"Aren't you the least bit curious why I'm here?"

"I'm more curious why you're still here."

Clint stared at the man, wondering what he had done before he won the election for sheriff, and where this aggressive attitude came from. One thing was clear, there

was no way Clint could have a civil conversation with
him, right now.

"Good day, Sheriff." Clint turned to leave.

"You leavin' town, Adams?"

"Right now I'm just leaving your office," Clint said.
"You see me around town and want me to leave town,
feel free to try."

"Just remember who the law in Lincoln is . . ." Eidson
was shouting, but Clint closed the door on him, cutting
him off.

Outside Clint shook his head and replayed the scene. Had
he overreacted to being called "old-timer"? He didn't
think so. The young lawman seemed to have an attitude
right away. Maybe he sensed Clint's surprise that a man
not yet thirty was wearing the sheriff's badge in Lincoln
County.

Whatever the reason, talking to the sheriff was out of
the question now.

He walked to Eclipse and untied the reins from the post.
Even when he'd been here during the whole Lincoln
County fracas he hadn't run into that kind of arrogance—
not even from Billy the Kid himself, who Clint remembered as a very polite young man.

Clint was in sort of a quandary about what to do next,
but when he spotted the Wortley Hotel across the street
he decided to go over there and see if Sam Wortley still
owned it. He had spent some pleasant evenings and nights
there with a slender, dark-haired, energetic girl named
Fiona, and it was as good a place as any to have a seat
and consider his options.

He walked over, tied Eclipse off in front and went inside.

"Room, sir?" the clerk asked.

"I thought I'd just have a seat and a beer," Clint said.

"Of course, sir. I'll get you that beer myself. Take a table."

Clint sat at a back table, in a corner, and waited while the clerk drew the beer and carried it over.

"Sam Wortley still own the place?"

"He does."

"You might tell him Clint Adams is out here enjoying one of his cold beers."

"I'll do that, sir."

"Oh, one thing," Clint said, as the clerk turned away.

"Sir?"

Clint felt silly asking, but he went ahead anyway.

"Which table was Bob Ollinger sitting at?"

The clerk, a tall, brown-haired, gentle-faced man said, "Many people ask that, sir. It was that one, near the fireplace. He was eating a roast beef dinner, and sitting with his back to the wall."

"Ah."

"When he heard someone shouting that Billy was escaping, he quickly ran out into the street and, well, met his demise."

"I know that part of the story, thanks," Clint said. "And thanks for the beer."

"Of course, sir," the man said. "My name is Tim. If you need anything else, just let me know."

"I will, thanks."

"And I will tell Mr. Wortley you're here."

"Thanks."

The clerk went back to work and Clint lingered over his beer and went back in mind to Lincoln County in a wilder, less controlled time . . .

PART TWO

FOURTEEN

Clint rolled over the next morning and bumped into Fiona, who barely stirred. They had gone at each other like animals for most of the night and she continued to snore even after being bumped. Clint's legs felt fatigued but he felt wide awake. The sun coming in through the window told him at was about nine A.M.

He got out of bed without waking her and got dressed. As he strapped on his gunbelt, she stirred and opened her eyes.

"Running out on me, Adams?"

"This is my room," Clint said. "You know where to find me."

She pushed herself up onto one elbow.

"I gotta go back to White Oaks. Belle only sent me over for one night."

"I see."

63

"If you wanna see me again," she explained, "you're gonna have to come over there."

"Belle's plan to get me back there."

"To get some money out of you."

Clint nodded. "Okay."

"Okay what?" She brushed some hair out of her eyes, allowing the sheet to slip down and reveal one soft, brown nipple.

"Okay, if I want to see you again, I'll come over there."

"Okay."

"Okay what?"

She shrugged. "Just okay."

"Okay," he said, and headed for the door. He almost had the door closed behind him when she spoke again.

"You won't have to pay."

He opened the door and looked back in. She was sitting up in bed, both breasts exposed.

"Okay." He closed the door.

He had breakfast downstairs in the bar, served to him by a waiter who turned out to be Sam Wortley, the owner of the hotel.

"Keeps my overhead down, doing a lot of these jobs myself," the man explained.

"I guess that's a smart business move."

"Let me know if you want more eggs."

Clint looked down at his plateful of eggs and half potatoes.

"Looks like I've got enough," he said. "You the cook, too?"

"Yup. The day it gets a little busier around here, maybe I'll hire more help. Enjoy your breakfast. I'll bring more coffee."

"Fine."

Wortley nodded and went back to the kitchen. Clint dug in and found the breakfast to be one of the best he'd ever had. When Wortley returned with more coffee, he told him so.

"Thanks. If I had my druthers I'd stay in the kitchen and let somebody else clerk and tend bar."

"A small businessman like yourself," Clint said, "you got any take on what's going on between, uh, Murphy-Dolan and Tunstall and, uh—"

"I know," Wortley said, sitting opposite Clint, "there are a lot of names involved. You askin' me what I think?" Wortley was in his forties, a sad-looking man with a seemingly outgoing personality. Clint was interested in his opinion.

"That's what I'm asking."

"I'm thinkin' Tunstall came here from England and stirred things up pretty good," Wortley said.

"You saying that was a bad thing?"

"Don't get me wrong," Wortley said. "I'm not in favor of monopolies. I believe in competition, but it seems to me in this case the safest bet would be to leave the status quo."

"That sort of sounds like riding the fence to me," Clint said. "From what I've heard the short time I've been in Lincoln County, most folks feel strongly one way or the other."

"Like you said," Wortley said, standing up, "I'm a small businessman. The outcome is really not going to affect me one way or the other. There are others who have more to lose—or gain."

"I guess so."

"More food?"

"No," Clint said, "I've had enough. It was great."

Wortley told him what he owed and he stood up, dug into his pocket and paid.

"You have any rooting interest in this business, Mr. . . ."

"Adams, Clint Adams," Clint said, "and no, I don't.

I'm not familiar with any of the parties involved."

"You The Gunsmith? That Adams?"

"That's right."

"Lookin' to hire out?"

"No," Clint said, "that's not what I'm looking for."

"Certain folks around here learn that you're here," Wortley said, "you'll get some offers—big money offers. A gun like yours could swing things to one side."

"Is that a fact?"

"You know that as well as I do," Wortley said, "that is, unless you're on the same side with Billy."

"Why's that?"

"Your gun and Billy's? Unbeatable."

"He's that good?"

"Don't know how he compares to you," Wortley said, "but he's the best I've seen around here."

"You've seen him handle a gun?"

"I have. He's very good."

"He as young as they say?"

"Oh, yeah," Wortley said. "He's a boy, but that gun makes him the same age as any man."

"Sounds like Billy the Kid is going to be interesting to meet."

"Depends which side of his gun you're on," Wortley said, and then added, "or which side of yours he's on."

Clint left the Wortley, crossed the street and started walking toward the Big Store. Standing outside he could see it was massive inside, and doing a brisk business. There appeared to be several people working behind three long counters, and he wondered if any of them were the owners.

Sam Wortley was right about one thing. The principals on either side were going to think he was looking to hire his gun out, or they were going to be bidding for his gun. That is, unless Chisum told Tunstall and McSween that he'd sent for him. He didn't think that was the case, though. Chisum appeared to want to remain in the background. Hiring Clint, or admitting to hiring him, would put him squarely in the foreground.

He squared his shoulders and entered the Big Store.

FIFTEEN

Clint browsed in the store while other customers were waited on. He was looking at soap when a man approached him and asked, "Can I help you?"

"Are you Mr. Riley?" Clint asked, pulling a name out of his hat.

"No," the man said, frowning, "I'm John Dolan. I am part owner of the store. And you are?"

Clint was stuck. He hadn't wanted to introduce himself so quickly, but he couldn't very well refuse to identify himself. He could have lied, but for what purpose?

"Clint Adams is my name."

Dolan studied him, then turned and said to one of the other clerks, "Darryl, I'll be in my office."

"Yes, sir," the young man replied, and went back to showing a woman some hats—possibly the latest Paris fashions.

"Will you come this way, please?"

Before Clint could even answer, Dolan started toward

the back of the store, and he had no choice but to follow.

"Have a seat," Dolan said, sitting behind a large oak desk that had seen only the best of care. Dolan fit the desk. He was easily in his fifties, but had seen only the best of care himself over the years and carried those years excellently. He had long sideburns and a well-tended mustache, and the part in his hair ran right down the middle. To his left, hanging on the wall, was an Army saber. Clint had no doubt that there was an Army Colt somewhere in the desk.

"I'm ex-Army, Mr. Adams, so I'm going to get right to the point. I heard you were in the area."

"You did?" Clint asked. "That's odd. I haven't really been here that long. In fact, last night was my first night."

"I have ways of getting information," Dolan said.

"Obviously."

"So you're either here looking for a job," Dolan said, "or you've got a job."

"What kind of job would that be?"

"Working for Tunstall," Dolan said. "If that's the case, you're either here to intimidate me, or kill me."

Dolan's hands were out of sight. That Army Colt Clint knew had to be in his desk could have been in his hand, at that moment. He hoped that Dolan was not a nervous man.

"Kill you? Right here in your office, with people outside? That wouldn't be very smart, would it?"

"There's a back door," Dolan said. "You could pull the trigger and be gone."

"Well, I guess I could," Clint said, "if that was why I was here."

"And it's not."

"No."

"Well," Dolan said, with a shrug of his shoulders, "good. Then that means you're for hire."

"Well, no," Clint said, "that's not the case, either—but

you can relax, Mr. Dolan. There's no need for that gun of yours to come into play."

"I was an officer in the Army, sir," Dolan said, "so I think I'll be the judge of that."

"Suit yourself."

"I will." His hands remained out of sight. "Tell me, then, why are you here?"

"Well . . . that's a little hard to say."

At that moment Dolan lifted his hands into sight, showing that they were both empty.

"It's a little early, but I'm going to have a brandy," he said. "Would you like one?"

"Yes," Clint said, "I believe I would."

SIXTEEN

John Tunstall looked up as Alex McSween entered the office behind their store.

"You don't look happy."

"I'm not," McSween said.

Tunstall put down his pencil and stared at his partner. McSween, in his thirties, was the older of the two, but there was never any question as to who the controlling partner was.

Tunstall folded his hands on top of the desk and said, "Come on. What's wrong?"

McSween sat down heavily across from his partner.

"I just heard some gossip."

"You know how I feel about gossip, Alex," Tunstall said. He was only twenty-three, but seemed wise and mature beyond his years. As far as McSween was concerned, it had a lot to do with that British accent.

"Well, this is more than gossip."

"Very well," Tunstall said. "Tell me."

"Clint Adams is in Lincoln County."

"And who is Clint Adams?"

McSween stared at his partner for a moment, then said, "Oh, I forgot, you're not from this country. Clint Adams is The Gunsmith."

"And why should it concern us that there is a new gunsmith in the county?"

"Not *a* gunsmith, John," McSween said, "*The* Gunsmith."

"What is the diff—Wait a moment," Tunstall said, as if something had suddenly occurred to him. "Why, I seem to recall the name now. Isn't the fellow some sort of . . . gunman?"

"Exactly," McSween said. "He's some sort of gunman. He's probably the fastest gun there is."

"Faster than our Billy?" Tunstall asked.

"I wouldn't want to put the boy to that kind of test right now," McSween said. "But it gets worse."

"How so?"

"I just saw a stranger walk into the Big Store."

"And you think it was The Gunsmith?"

"I'm sure of it."

"Have you ever seen him before?"

"Just some pictures in the newspaper," McSween said, "but this looked like him."

"So you think he's going to work for Dolan?"

"I think we're in trouble if he does."

"Well then," Tunstall said, "we just have to approach this like any other business decision."

"How's that?"

"We'll have to make him a better offer."

"Whatever offer Tunstall and McSween make to you," J. J. Dolan said to Clint, "or will make to you, we'll better."

"I told you, Mr. Dolan," Clint said, "I'm not here looking for a job."

"That's the second or third time you've told me why you're *not* here," Dolan said. "Why don't you tell me why you *are* here?"

Clint finished his brandy and laid the fragile glass firmly on the edge of Dolan's desk. He still wasn't sure what his answer was going to be.

"I guess I have to plead curiosity," he finally said.

"What?"

"Well," Clint went on, "I was just passing through, really, when I started hearing all this talk of trouble brewing. I kept hearing that the owners of these two stores were also competitors for some Army contracts for cattle and horses, and that the competition was going to turn violent."

Dolan stared at Clint for a few moments without comment.

"You expect me to believe that?" he asked then. "Just passing through."

Clint spread his hands and said, "That's the way it was."

"All right," Dolan said, "I'll play your game. Yes, there's competition going on. We were here first. That is, Lawrence Murphy was first, and then my partner, John Riley, and I bought the store from Murphy. Tunstall is a young upstart from another country who came here to cut into our profits. Will it get violent? Probably, because Tunstall is hiring young gunmen like Billy the Kid and Charlie Bowdre and others."

"And you don't have any hired guns on your side?"

"We have the law on our side, Mr. Adams," Dolan said, "although, as I said, we're not averse to laying out some money—"

"I'm just looking to satisfy my curiosity, Mr. Dolan,"

Clint said. "So you think this thing is going to come to gunplay?"

"It's got to," Dolan said. "I'm not about to let someone just come in and cut into my profits."

"You don't see another way out?"

"Yes, I do," Dolan said. "Tunstall packs up and goes back to England, and McSween packs up and goes back to being a lawyer somewhere else. I'm not about to let some young limey upstart, a lawyer and a wet-behind-the-ears gunny . . . Well, I think I've made my point."

Dolan sat back and regarded Clint silently, calming himself.

"I guess that answers my questions." He started to stand.

"Wait." Dolan took out a piece of paper and wrote a number down on it, then pushed it across to Clint.

"What's this?" Clint asked.

"A signing bonus," Dolan said. "We can talk salary later."

Clint picked up the slip of paper and looked at the number.

"That's very generous."

"I think so," Dolan said. "Just think it over."

"Your partner will go along with this?"

"I make most of the decisions, Mr. Adams," Dolan said.

Clint figured Dolan wasn't quite finished being an "officer" in the Army.

"I'll keep it mind," Clint said, standing.

"I assume you'll be talking to Tunstall and McSween," Dolan said. "Listen to both offers and make up your mind. We'll talk again."

Clint decided not to protest any longer.

SEVENTEEN

Clint left the store and stopped just outside. How could he expect anyone to believe that he was asking all these questions just out of curiosity? Maybe he'd be better served by acting like he actually was trying to decide which side to work for. At least they'd be more frank with him that way. In the end, that was the impression he left Dolan with, that he was considering his options. He decided to take that same tack with Tunstall and see what he could learn.

Although he was being paid by Chisum, he was actually doing this mostly as a favor to the man. They weren't great friends, but it never hurt to have a man with that much power indebted to you. If he could figure out a way to avoid a violent conflict in Lincoln County, he'd have a huge favor coming in return.

The Tunstall store was farther down the street, and when Clint Adams entered both the Brit and his partner, McSween, were stationed behind a counter. Tunstall had decided that if McSween was right and Adams was in with Dolan, then his next stop would be logical.

When Clint walked in, McSween gave Tunstall the high sign that this was the man he'd seen entering Dolan's store. The two partners had already agreed that if this was indeed Adams and he was there to "interview" for a job, they would conduct that interview together.

When Clint walked in and saw the young, well-dressed man behind the desk, he immediately decided that this had to be Tunstall. If nothing else, the three-piece suit and starched collar gave him away as a non-Westerner. He saw a look pass between the two men and assumed that the other was McSween. There appeared to be about a ten-year difference in their ages.

The Tunstall store was not as large, nor was it as busy at the Dolan store had been. Clint decided to do away with phony browsing and just address the two men, especially since they were alone in the store.

"Mr. McSween? Mr. Tunstall?"

"I'm McSween," the older man said.

"Mr. Adams, I presume?" Tunstall asked.

"That's right," Clint said. "I see word gets around fast."

"Did Mr. Dolan know you were coming?"

"He had heard I was around. I assume you heard the same thing? You fellas all seem to keep your ears to the ground."

Tunstall looked at McSween, as if he didn't recognize the reference.

"He means we keep our ears open and hear things," McSween translated.

"I see," Tunstall replied. "Yes, we tend to know what's going on around us. What kind of offer did Dolan make? Or are you already in his employ?"

"I'm not in anyone's employ, at the moment."

"That is good," Tunstall said, "then you're prepared to hear our offer."

"I'm more interested in hearing how this whole affair started," Clint said.

Tunstall frowned. "Why?"

"I'm just wondering if violence can be avoided."

That made Tunstall frown even more.

"Why would a gunman like yourself want violence averted?" he asked. "Isn't violence your business?"

"As a matter of fact," Clint said, "it's not."

"John," McSween said, "why don't we humor Mr. Adams and answer his questions? Maybe that'll help him make up his mind."

"Well," Tunstall said, "we don't have any customers . . . why not?"

"What do you want to know, Mr. Adams?" McSween asked.

"I'd simply like to know," Clint said, "if there's another way to resolve this conflict, without gunplay and bloodshed?"

Tunstall just shook his head, confused. To his mind Clint was a hired gun, and he didn't understand why he'd want to talk anything else but price.

"Well," McSween said, "as a lawyer I'm always ready to try to talk things out and find an easy resolution."

"So you would sit down and talk with Dolan and Riley?" Clint asked.

"If they were willing."

"Which they are not," Tunstall said. "You've already spoken with one of them, I assume. Was it Dolan?"

"Yes."

"Did he give you the speech about being an ex–Army officer?"

"He mentioned it."

"He would," Tunstall said. "He thinks he still is an officer, and that everyone should follow orders like good little soldiers. Well, I am not a good little soldier, Mr. Adams. All I have done is to try to carve out a living for myself in your country, because this was where I had heard the opportunity was. Mr. Dolan, on the other hand, has done nothing but threaten me—us—with violence ever since we started our business here. I believe everyone has a right to make a living in this country?"

"That's what they tell me."

"Well, Mr. Dolan does not feel the same way. We tried to talk to him in the beginning, but he would have none of it. He tried to use the law against us, but Sheriff Brady is nothing but a joke. When we heard that he had begun to amass a force of men, we began gathering our own."

"The Regulators?"

"That is what I call them, yes."

"Sounds like you're hiring them pretty young, Mr. Tunstall."

"There's nothing wrong with young men trying to make their way, is there, Mr. Adams?"

"No, I suppose not," Clint said. He looked at McSween, but the man had subsided and left the stage to his partner. Before any of them could speak, though, a woman entered the store and stopped just inside.

"Oh, I'm sorry," she said, "I didn't know you were busy."

She was pretty, blonde, in her early twenties, and she obviously knew the two partners.

"Oh, darling," McSween said. "No, it's all right. You can come in. We were just . . . talking. Mr. Adams, this is my wife, Susan McSween."

"Ma'am," Clint said, tipping his hat.

"Mr. Adams is here interviewing for a position, my dear," Tunstall told her.

"Really?" She looked Clint up and down with pretty blue eyes. "You don't look like a store clerk."

"He's not," McSween said.

"That is not the position he is applying for," Tunstall said.

"Oh," Susan said, and then she caught on and said, "Oh," again, in an entirely different tone of voice.

"Actually, Mrs. McSween," Clint said, "I'm not really applying for any position. We were just . . . talking about the situation here in Lincoln."

"Talking?" She looked confused. After all, Clint did look more like a gunman than a clerk, and she was sure that was what Tunstall was referring to. But he also seemed a little old to be one of Tunstall's Regulators. Her husband and his partner had been hiring younger men up to this point. Although, even she could see that having a man of experience would not be a bad thing.

"Well," Clint said, "I think I've taken up enough of your time, gentlemen," Clint said. He touched his hat. "Ma'am."

She nodded to him and moved to stand by her husband. Tunstall came from around the counter and walked Clint outside. Once there he put his hand out and Clint took it, even though he knew this was a ruse to make it seem they had come to some sort of agreement.

"Come back when you're ready to hear my offer," Tunstall said to him. "I'm sure you'll find it competitive."

"I'm sure I would."

He turned to leave, then turned back suddenly.

"You have a young man named Bonney in your employ."

"William," Tunstall said. "Yes, he's an important part of my . . . of our business."

"Is he? I've been hearing interesting things about him."

"He's an interesting young man," Tunstall said. "Quite the dancer, I hear."

"Dancer?"

"Yes," the Brit said, "at least, that is the reputation he has. Were you speaking of some other . . . talent?"

"Good day, Mr. Tunstall," Clint said. "Thanks for talking with me."

EIGHTEEN

The handshake with Tunstall in front of his store did not go unnoticed. John Riley was standing across the street when it happened and he hurried back to his own store to tell his partner, Dolan.

"Right in front of everyone," he said, still out of breath from running back.

"It doesn't mean anything, John," J. J. Dolan said. "It's just the kind of stunt Tunstall would pull. I made Adams a hell of an offer. He'll come around."

"I hope so," Riley said. "I don't see our men wanting to face Billy and Clint Adams."

"It won't come to that," Dolan said. "I think we can do something about Billy."

"And Adams?"

Dolan smiled.

"If he does come around, maybe he's what we can do about Billy," he said.

• • •

"What was that all about?" Susan McSween asked both her husband and Tunstall.

"I'll leave your husband to explain it to you," the young Brit said, and went back to the office.

"What's he gotten you into now, Alex?" she demanded after Tunstall had left.

"Nothing, darling," McSween said.

"Who was that man?"

"His name is Clint Adams."

Her eyes widened.

"The Gunsmith?"

"The same."

"Is he going to work for you?"

"We don't know."

"Not for Dolan and Riley!"

"I said we don't know, Susan."

"Well, make him an offer, Alex. You can't let him go over to their side. I know he's older than the others you and John have been hiring, but he's also experienced."

"I know that," McSween said. "Look, Susan, John and I will handle it. It's our business."

"It's my business, too, Alex," she reminded him. "Don't forget that."

"Susan," McSween said, "John and I will handle it."

"What does Mr. Chisum say?"

"We haven't talked to Chisum."

"But he can help," she said, "he can advise you—"

"Chisum's a silent partner, Susan, you know that," McSween reminded her. "All he's done is put up some money to back us. He wants to stay in the background."

"I don't see what harm there could be in asking his advice."

"Shhh. Keep your voice down."

"Are you afraid that Tunstall will hear your wife having an idea, Alex?" she demanded. "Or talking back to you? Does he think I should be the quiet little woman? Hmm?"

"Susan—"

"My god, Alex, he's barely older than Billy!"

"He has experience despite his youth, Susan—"

"I'm going shopping!" she snapped. She headed for the door, then turned and added, "And not here! You get Clint Adams on our side, Alex. You hear me? Get him!"

McSween watched helplessly as his wife walked out. It was true, Tunstall did expect Susan to be the quiet little woman, but he'd never tell her that. The Lord only knew what she'd do to Tunstall if he did.

NINETEEN

Clint rode from Lincoln out to John Chisum's ranch. There he was greeted by the foreman, Johnny Boggs.

"Johnny," he said, dismounting.

"Want your horse taken care of?"

"I don't expect to be here that long," Clint said. "Why don't you just leave him out here?"

"Boss expecting you?"

"I would think he'd always be expecting me."

"I'll take you in, then."

Clint followed Boggs up the stairs of the big house to the porch and front door.

"Johnny, have you met Billy the Kid?"

Boggs stopped short of opening the front door and turned around to face Clint.

"We've spoken."

"What's he like?"

Boggs shrugged. "Young, full of himself."

"Arrogant?"

"That comes with being young, doesn't it?"

"Foolish?"

"Also fits the description."

"I guess," Clint said. "What about the other Regulators?"

"I know some of them," Boggs said, "Charlie Bowdre, obviously. Henry Brown, Frank McNab, Jim French, some of the others. They're all good boys, I think."

"Young, like Billy?"

"Not as young as Billy, but young."

"They all look up to him, though?"

"I guess. Billy's the one with the forceful personality," Boggs explained. "People tend to like him,"

"How did he meet Tunstall?"

"Rode against Tunstall for a while, then realized he was on the wrong side. I'm not sure who sought who out, but he ended up working for him."

"Loyal to him?"

"Pretty much. You talk to Tunstall?"

Clint nodded. "And McSween." He went on to explain that he had pretty much spoken to all the principals, except for Murphy.

"Murphy's pretty much out of it."

"I gathered that."

"I'll take you in to the boss before you say any more you'll have to repeat."

Boggs went to open the door, then stopped again.

"Clint?"

"Yeah?"

"I work for Chisum," he said. "Even though my boss backed Tunstall and McSween, I don't work for them."

"I understand."

"But I'll do anything that will benefit Mr. Chisum." He'd been speaking over his shoulder up to then, but turned to look at Clint. "Do you understand what I'm saying?"

"I think I do," Clint said. "I can count on you to back me as long as I'm acting for Mr. Chisum."

"Okay," Boggs said. "We understand each other, then."

"We do."

Boggs nodded, and opened the door.

This time when Clint sat across from Chisum in the man's office Johnny Boggs stayed.

"I didn't expect results this quickly," Chisum said.

"No results," Clint said, "just a quick report on my progress."

He explained about his conversations with the parties involved, and whatever else he had learned by keeping his ears open in Lincoln, Carrizozo and White Oaks.

"Johnny told me about the poker game, and how you kept him from killing Charlie Bowdre."

"Is that how he put it?" Clint didn't look over at Boggs.

"No, but I know that if you hadn't stopped Bowdre from drawing his gun Johnny would have killed him."

Clint filed that away for future reference. Chisum's endorsement of Johnny Boggs carried some weight.

"John," Clint said, "I don't know what I can do for you here. Both sides seem intent on their goals, which are obviously at odds. They're going to come to blows."

Chisum sat back in his chair and stared at the ceiling.

"I know this is going to happen," he said, finally, "but . . ." He lowered his head and stared at Clint. "Can you stay around awhile? I'll pay you for your time."

"John—"

"You don't have to be anywhere else, do you?"

"I have nothing pressing," Clint said. "I just don't think I can do anything . . . helpful . . ."

"I'll owe you, big time."

Which was the reason he had come in the first place.

"Bigger," Clint said.

"Right," Chisum said, "I'll owe you bigger than I al-

ready do. Look, just stay around, sample what Little Casino has to offer in White Oaks. Stay at the Wortley—"

"How'd you know I'm at the Wortley?"

"I have eyes and ears," Chisum said.

Meaning Sam Wortley, probably.

"Just hang around, play some poker, sample the girls,
walk around, be seen . . . I don't know," Chisum said. "I'll
just feel better if you stay around."

Clint looked over at Johnny Boggs, who shrugged.

"Poker sounds good to me," Clint said, with a shrug.

He looked back at Chisum and said, "I'll stay—for a
while."

"That's all I ask," Chisum said. "Thanks. Do you need
some money?"

"No, I'm fine," Clint said, "although if I decide to shop
in that Big Store I'll probably need some. I noticed how
high their prices are."

"You'd think they'd both lower their prices, since
they're competing, right?"

Clint stood up, followed by Chisum, who offered his
hand.

"Seems like you've met everyone but Billy," he said,
as they shook hands.

"And the rest of the Regulators."

"The rest don't matter," Chisum said. "They'll follow
Billy."

"You think I should meet him?"

"No," Chisum said, "you'd be too big a target for him.
He wouldn't be able to resist. My advice is stay away
from Billy."

Clint wondered which of them John Chisum thought he
was protecting.

TWENTY

"Do you know who the guy was?" William Bonney asked Charlie Bowdre.

"No," Bowdre said. "All I know is he stuck his nose in my business."

"He was in the game, too, right?'

"So?"

"Sounds to me like what went on was his business."

The two young Regulators were in the bunkhouse of the Flying H Ranch owned by John Tunstall.

"Charlie, what were you thinkin'?" Billy the Kid asked. "Didn't Mr. Tunstall tell us to stay out of trouble?"

"I wasn't lookin' for trouble, Billy," Charlie said. "I was just tryin' to play some cards."

"Charlie," Billy said, "you're terrible at poker, don't you know that by now?"

"I ain't," Bowdre said.

"You always lose."

"I just have bad luck," Bowdre said, "combined with bad cards."

"You stink, Charlie."

Billy Bonney was rather slight, not tall; he really did not have a commanding physical presence, and yet he commanded the respect of all the other Regulators. Bowdre felt bad that Billy thought he was a bad poker player.

"That's just mean, Billy."

"Come on, Charlie," Billy said, "forget it."

"I ain't gonna forget it, Billy," Bowdre said. "Both Johnny Boggs and the stranger owe me money."

"Mr. Chisum ain't gonna like it if you kill his foreman, Sweet Johnny," Billy pointed out.

At that point two of the other Regulators came in.

"What's goin' on?" Jim French asked.

"What are you fellas doin'?" Fred Wyat asked.

Both men were in their twenties, about the same age as Bowdre. While Billy was not yet twenty, they all looked to him as their leader, and they all preferred to be in his presence, especially when riding into White Oak. The girls loved to be around Billy.

"I'm tryin' to keep Charlie from killin' Johnny Boggs."

"Whataya got against Sweet Johnny, Charlie?" Wyat asked. "He's okay."

"Johnny took some of Charlie's money in poker," Billy explained.

"Charlie," French said, "you shouldn't play poker."

"I play better than you!"

"Yeah, you do," French said, "but I know I'm a bad poker player."

"You can all go to hell!" Bowdre stood up, grabbed his hat and headed for the door.

"What's got him so hot and bothered?" Wyat asked.

"Don't worry about him," Billy said, "but he did say something interesting."

"Like what?" French asked.

"There's a stranger in town who kept Charlie from killin' Johnny," Billy said.

"Who is he?" Wyat asked.

Billy stared at him. "If I knew that he wouldn't be a stranger, would he?"

"Dummy," French said.

"Get Frank and some of the others," Billy told them. "Cover Lincoln and White Oaks, Carrizozo too."

"For what?" Wyat asked.

"I want to know who this stranger is," Billy said. "And I want to know who he works for."

"You think Dolan and Riley hired him?"

"If he worked for Mr. Tunstall," Billy said, "we'd know about it, wouldn't we?"

"So what?" French asked. "They have other guys workin' for them, like Morton and—"

"I don't care about them," Billy said. "I know all of them and what they can do. This stranger I don't know, and he made a fool out of Charlie last night."

"That ain't hard," Wyat said, laughing and nudging French.

"Find out who he is," Billy said.

"And what are you gonna do?" French asked Billy.

"Me? I'm gonna do what Mr. Tunstall asked us to do. I'm gonna stay out of trouble."

TWENTY-ONE

Clint left the Chisum house with Johnny Boggs walking him out. They paused before Clint mounted Eclipse.

"You think it's going to be easy for me to stay away from Billy?" Clint asked him.

"I think Billy already heard about you from Charlie Bowdre," Boggs said. "The question is, does he know your name yet?"

"If he doesn't, he soon will, right?"

"Oh yeah."

"Do you agree with Chisum?"

"About you being a big target for Billy? Oh yeah, but you also have to remember how loyal Billy is to Tunstall."

"So you think that would keep Billy from coming after me?"

"Billy'll leave you alone until he knows which side you're on."

"And if I'm not on either side?"

"Then you're a target," Boggs said. "As long as you're working for Mr. Chisum, though—"

"I consider this more of a favor to Chisum," Clint said, cutting him off.

"He's going to pay you, though."

"I haven't decided yet whether to take money from him, so for now it's a favor."

Boggs thought that over then said, "Seems to me having Chisum in your debt might be better than getting paid."

"I was thinking that, too."

Clint climbed aboard Eclipse and gathered up the reins.

"See you in White Oaks?" Boggs asked.

"Where else would I go for some excitement?" Clint asked.

"Well, there are saloons in Carrizozo and Lincoln," Boggs said, "or you could go to Roswell, or even all the way up to Las Vegas, but actually White Oaks is the place to be."

"For excitement," Clint asked, "or for trouble?"

"Both. If you run into Billy, it'll probably be in White Oaks."

"And what about you, with Bowdre?"

"The time will come between me and Charlie," Boggs said, "but I think you'll have to watch out for him, too. I'll tell you one thing for sure, though."

"What's that?"

"When and if Billy comes, he'll come alone," Boggs said, "but Bowdre, he'll bring help."

"That's good to know," Clint said. "Chisum seems to have a lot of confidence in you, Johnny. That's good to know, too."

"If I'm going to back you, I'll be there, Clint," Boggs said. "You can count on it."

"I will."

"Just remember," Boggs said, with a grin, "at the poker table, it's every man for himself."

"I wouldn't have it any other way," Clint said.

TWENTY-TWO

Clint went back to Lincoln, intending to return to White Oaks later that evening. As he entered the Wortley, the owner, Sam, came over and called his name.

"Thought I should warn you, there was some Regulators here asking about you.'

"Regulators?"

"The ones workin' for Tunstall."

Clint decided not to tell Wortley he already knew about the Regulators.

"What did they want?"

"They said they heard there was a stranger in town, and wanted to know if he was stayin' here."

"They didn't ask for me by name?"

"No," Wortley said, "the impression I got was that they were tryin' to find out your name."

"What did you tell them?"

"I told them I don't talk about my guests."

"Did they take that well?"

"Those boys don't scare me none," Wortley said, puffing out his chest. "They know that."

"And they probably know you're friends with John Chisum, right?" Clint asked.

"Chisum? Uh, him and me, we're on the town council together, but—"

"It's okay, Mr. Wortley," Clint said, "I know you told Chisum I'm staying here, but I appreciate you not giving the Regulators any information."

"Are you workin' for Dolan, Mr. Adams?" Wortley asked. "Is that why they're lookin' for you?"

"I'm not working for Dolan or Tunstall, Mr. Wortley," Clint said, "and I don't know why they were looking for me. Maybe they're just curious about strangers."

"Well, just so's you know," Wortley said, "Billy wasn't with them, but I heard them talkin'. They said Billy wants to find out who the stranger was who embarrassed Charlie Bowdre in White Oaks."

"I see," Clint said. "Well, thanks, Mr. Wortley."

"You can just call me Sam," Wortley said. "Everybody does."

"Okay, Sam," Clint said, "thanks for the warning."

"You watch out for them boys, Mr. Adams," Wortley said. "Some of them are just plain mean. Not Billy, mind you."

"He's not mean?"

"No, sir," Wortley said, "A bit rash, maybe, but not mean like some of the others."

"Okay, Sam," Clint said, "I'll keep this all in mind . . . and listen, you can just call me Clint."

"Yes, sir!" Wortley said, "I mean, Clint. You want a beer? You look like you been riding."

"Yeah, thanks, Sam," Clint said. "That's actually what I came in here for."

He followed Wortley to the bar where the man drew him a cold one.

"Sam, there was a lady in my room when I left this morning," Clint said.

"Yeah, I saw her leave," Wortley said, with a big smile. "Real pretty, she was. One of Madam Varnish's girls?"

"Yes," Clint said. "Did she, uh, say anything when she left?"

"Naw," Wortley said, "I just saw her through the window."

"Okay, thanks," Clint said. "I'm going to take this out on the porch to drink."

"Fine by me . . . Clint."

Clint raised the mug to the man and then carried it outside, where he pulled a straight-backed wooden chair up to the wall and sat down. It occurred to him that the Regulators who were looking for him might come walking by, but there was no use in hiding from anybody. Sooner or later they'd find out his name and report it back to Billy. Clint wondered why Billy didn't just ask Tunstall or Chisum if they knew?

He assumed Billy was trying to find out who he was just as a matter of identifying a stranger in town. Since he seemed to be the leader of the Regulators, it made sense for him to want to know who was new in town. After all, every newcomer was a potential new player in the drama that was taking place in Lincoln County. It was simply the smart thing to do, which told him that Billy was smart, in addition to everything else he'd learned about him.

Clint continued to work on his beer slowly as he watched the street in front of him. There wasn't much else for him to do, at the moment. After all, Chisum had simply asked him to "hang around," and that's what he was doing.

TWENTY-THREE

Clint spent the next few days the same way, sitting on the porch in front of the Wortley, walking around town, spending time at the Little Casino in White Oaks, playing poker with Johnny Boggs and others, and then either going with Fiona to her room or taking her back to the Wortley with him. True to her word, she never charged him. He didn't know how this sat with Belle La Mar, and he didn't ask.

What he didn't know was that he had finally been identified to Billy the Kid, whose eyes widened when he got the word who the stranger in town was.

It was actually another of the Regulators, Henry Brown, who found out because he was sleeping with one of Belle La Mar's girls—and paying—who was friends with Fiona, and the two girls had discussed the fact that Fiona was spending time with Clint Adams.

"The Gunsmith," Billy said, his eyes taking on a hungry look.

"You gonna try him, Billy?" Jim French asked.

"He's got to try him," Charlie Bowdre said. "He might never get another chance like this. Right, Billy?"

"Shut up, Charlie," Billy said. "I gotta think."

Later that day Billy went into Lincoln. By this time Clint had left the Wortley porch and ridden over to White Oaks. Billy went in the Tunstall store to talk with his boss.

"Billy," McSween said, as the boy walked in. "What brings you here?"

"I wanna talk to Mr. Tunstall, Mr. McSween," Billy said. While he respected both men, and was loyal to both, he had stronger feelings for Tunstall, perhaps because they were closer in age.

"He's in the office," McSween said. "Is there something I can help you with?"

"No, sir," Billy said. "I just wanted to talk with Mr. Tunstall."

"Well, go on back, then," McSween said. "He won't mind."

"Thank you."

As McSween watched the young man walk to the back of the store, he knew that, while Billy had been as polite as ever, there was something going on inside the boy. Suddenly, McSween knew what it was. He must have found out that The Gunsmith was in town. That would explain that look in his eye.

Billy the Kid was thinking about doing something foolish. McSween hoped that Tunstall would be able to rein him in, because the lawyer wasn't at all sure that Billy could take Clint Adams.

Tunstall called out "Come," when someone knocked on his office door. When he saw Billy enter, he sat back and ignored the papers on his desk. He had an enormous liking for Billy, and was always glad to see him.

"Come in, William, come in," he said. "To what do I owe the pleasure of an afternoon visit from my favorite Regulator?"

Billy removed his hat out of respect for his employer and said, "Well, Mr. Tunstall, I hear tell Clint Adams is in town."

"Yes, I know."

"Did you send for The Gunsmith, sir?" Billy asked. "Is he workin' for you?"

"No, William," Tunstall said, "he is most certainly not working for me."

"Then is he workin' for Dolan?"

"Actually," Tunstall said, "I've spoken with Mr. Adams. He came here to see me."

"To sell his gun?"

"One would assume that."

"Then he hasn't hired on with Dolan?"

"He is not working for Dolan or me, William."

"Then . . . what's he doing in Lincoln?"

"I don't know."

"Are you gonna try to hire him?"

Tunstall sat back in his chair.

"Do you think I should?" he asked.

"No, sir," Billy said. "Me and the boys can handle anything that comes along."

"And what do you think is going to come along, William?"

"Gunplay," Billy said. "Bloodshed."

"Do you really expect that?"

"Ain't no avoidin' it, sir."

"Then wouldn't you want to have someone like The Gunsmith on your side?"

"I can only have boys backin' me I can trust, Mr. Tunstall," Billy said. "I don't know this fella, and I can't trust him."

"Well then, shouldn't I try to hire him just so he doesn't hire on with Dolan and Riley?"

"No, sir. If you don't want him to hire on with them, you just give me the word."

"And what will you do?"

"I'll take care of him."

"Isn't that what this is about, William?" Tunstall asked. "You want to test your mettle against the Gunsmith."

"Well, sir," Billy said, "I don't know what you mean by 'metal,' but if you mean I want to try my gun against him, well then you got it right."

"William," Tunstall said, "you don't need to test yourself against this man to prove anything."

"I'm sorry, Mr. Tunstall," Billy said, 'but I wouldn't be much of a man if I didn't want to try him. I mean, what man in his right mind who thinks he's good with a gun wouldn't?"

Tunstall considered the question for a few moments before speaking again.

"William," he said, "for the time being I am going to have to ask you to stay away from Clint Adams. Is that understood?"

Billy worried his hat in his hands and asked, "Is that an order, Mr. Tunstall?"

"Have I ever ordered you around, William?"

"No, sir."

"You pledged your allegiance to me, did you not?"

"Yes, sir?"

"And promised to do as I asked?"

"Yes, sir, I did."

"Then I'm not ordering you now, William," Tunstall said. "I am asking you. Please do not go near The Gunsmith."

"For how long, sir?"

"Until I tell you to."

"So you're sayin' the time will come?"

"William," Tunstall said, "with you and Clint Adams both in Lincoln County, I believe it is unavoidable."

After Billy the Kid left, McSween went into the office to talk with Tunstall.

"Did you convince him to stay away from Adams?"

"You knew, eh?"

"I could see it in his eyes when he walked in."

"I suppose we could let him go ahead and kill him, but that would just start trouble, wouldn't it?"

"And it might get Billy killed."

"You don't think he can take Adams?"

"John," McSween said, "Clint Adams just might be the fastest gun alive."

"Would you tell William that?" Tunstall asked. "To his face?"

"I don't have a death wish."

"He would never raise his gun to you."

"Not to you, maybe," McSween said. "I'm not so sure about me."

"Well then," Tunstall said, "As long as I have William's ear, he will not raise his gun to you, Adams or anyone . . . until I say so."

"And when would that be, John?"

"I'm not sure, Alex," Tunstall said. "I am going to have to think about this for quite some time."

TWENTY-FOUR

Clint wondered why he hadn't run into Charlie Bowdre over the next few days, across the poker table. The only thing he could think was that Bowdre had been warned to stay away from him—or from Boggs, or from any combination of the two. Clint played poker with Boggs twice, and they both won money from the other players in pretty much equal amounts.

On the fifth night after he agreed to "hang around," Clint was at the bar with Boggs following a game.

"Billy knows who you are," Boggs said.

"That was inevitable," Clint said. "How do you know?"

"He told Tunstall, Tunstall told Chisum, Chisum told me. He also asked me to watch your back."

"Instead of doing your regular job?"

"No," Boggs said, "only when we're in the same place at the same time, like now."

"Guess I'll have to watch my own back the rest of the time."

"Billy's not going to try you."

"Why not?"

"He's been told not to."

"By who?"

"Tunstall," Boggs said, and then added, "Well, not told, exactly. More like asked."

"And does Billy usually do what Tunstall asks him to?"

"Always."

"Then I guess I'm okay, for a while," Clint said, "until Tunstall decides to send Billy after me."

"Why would he do that?"

Clint shrugged. "Maybe he'll come to think I'm working for Dolan—that is, unless Chisum told him why I'm here."

"No," Boggs said. "Chisum hasn't said a word."

"So I'm in my own."

"Except for me," Boggs said, raising his beer mug.

"Except for you." Clint raised his mug, as well.

"Sweet Johnny," the blonde, Starla, said, coming up behind Boggs and sliding her arms around his waist.

"Hello, Starla."

She moved around so that she was standing in front of him, her arms still around his waist. Clint could smell her perfume.

"Are you coming upstairs with me tonight?"

"No, honey, not tonight," Johnny said. "Why don't you take Clint, here?"

"Him?" Starla asked, looking at Clint over her shoulder with a flirtatious smile. "He's private stock."

"What?"

"Fi-o-na," Starla said, pronouncing it very carefully.

"Ah."

She made a face and said, "Guess I'll have to go find ol' Henry Brown."

Johnny kissed her on the nose and said, "Sorry."

She moved away and Clint asked, "Henry Brown?"

"One of the Regulators," Johnny said, "so not really very old. Kinda dirty, but not old. He likes Starla."

"But does Starla like him?"

"She doesn't have to," Boggs said. "It's her job."

"But she likes you?"

"Of course."

"How do you know that?"

"I know when a woman likes me."

"Sure."

"Besides," Johnny Boggs said, "I'm clean."

That's when Clint saw it, that "Sweet" Johnny Boggs smile. He thought the man had more teeth than anyone he'd ever seen before.

"I guess that counts," Clint said, "even to a whore."

Boggs finished his beer and set the empty on the bar.

"Another?" the bartender asked.

"Nope," Boggs said. "Gotta go." He looked at Clint. "Keep watching your back."

"I never stop."

Boggs nodded and left.

"How about you?" the barman asked. " 'Nother?"

Clint looked down at the half inch or so he had left, drained it and asked, "Why not?"

TWENTY-FIVE

In a back room of the Murphy-Dolan-Riley store Deputy Sheriff William Morton was meeting with Tom Hill, several other men, and J. J. Dolan.

Except that Morton was not really a deputy.

"You are now," Dolan said. He took a deputy sheriff's badge from the top drawer of his desk and tossed it at Morton, who grabbed for it and missed. It hit the floor with a metallic clatter. Morton bent down and picked it up, stared at it.

"Pin it on," Dolan said. "Consider yourself sworn in."

"Yes, sir." Morton, a big, florid-faced man in his forties, did as he was told.

"Now listen closely, all of you," Dolan said. "Tunstall has some horses that don't belong to him. You're all gonna go out to his ranch tomorrow and attach them."

"Attach?" one man asked.

"Take them," Tom Hill said. He was a tall, slender cowboy from one of the ranches along the Rio Pecos. He was eager to get into J. J. Dolan's good graces.

"That's right," Dolan said. "You'll take them."

"Tunstall won't just let us take them," Morton pointed out.

"You will be a duly appointed officer of the law," Dolan said, "within your rights to attach the horses, no matter what."

"Yes, sir."

"Tunstall will probably resist," Dolan said. "In fact, I'm hoping he'll resist."

"And if he does?" Morton asked.

"If he does, you'll use force."

"How much force?" the "deputy" asked.

"As much as necessary," Dolan said. He hesitated, then added, "Do you all understand?"

Some did but some didn't. However, they all nodded. The ones who didn't understand would later ask the ones who did to explain.

"All right," Dolan said, "I want you all to leave but Morton and Hill."

Hill's chest puffed up at being singled out. The other men filed out and closed the door behind them. Already men were asking other men for an explanation.

"I want to make things clear to the two of you," Dolan said. "I want Tunstall dead."

"What if Billy and the others are there?" Morton asked.

"You'll outnumber them."

"How do you know that?"

"I know," Dolan said. "Besides, I don't think Billy will be there."

"And how do you know that?" Morton asked.

"I don't," Dolan said. "I said I 'think', didn't I?"

"Yes, sir."

"We'll take care of it, sir," Hill said. "You don't have to worry."

"Another thing," Dolan said.

"What?" Morton asked.

"Riley doesn't know anything about this."

"And Murphy?" Morton asked.

"Murphy doesn't know anything anymore," Dolan said. "This is my play."

"What about Sheriff Brady?" Morton asked. "What's going to be his position?"

"You're one of his deputies," Dolan said. "He'll back you."

"If you say so."

"Oh, don't worry," Dolan said. "He will."

Dolan opened the top drawer of his desk again and took out three envelopes.

"This one is yours," he said, handing one to Morton, "and this one is yours," he said, handing another to Hill. "This third one gets split up among the other men." Morton nodded, and took that one.

"Okay, Morton," Dolan said. "You can go. I want to talk to Hill."

Morton frowned, but said, "Yes, sir."

"Pay the men after the job is done. Understand?"

"Yes, sir."

Dolan waited for Morton to leave and close the door behind him.

"Tom," he said, then, "this is what I want you to do . . ."

The next morning Tunstall was on his ranch with three of his men. He was standing on the ground, his horse a few feet away, the reins grounded. The men with him were ranch hands, and not Regulators. They were working with some horses when a group of men rode up on them. The sun glinted off the badge on one of their chests.

"Boss?" one of the men said.

Tunstall turned and saw the men approaching.

"Law," another man said.

Suddenly, the approaching men pulled their guns.

"Law with their guns out!" one of the other men said. He turned and ran, and that panicked the rest of the men, who ran off as well, leaving Tunstall alone.

The Englishman turned to face the approaching group which, with a lawman in the lead, appeared to be a posse. Tunstall was not wearing a sidearm, and his rifle was on his horse.

He stood still, waiting.

Morton led Hill and the other men toward Tunstall, who was standing alone as his men ran off.

"No Regulators," Hill said.

"And no Billy," Morton said.

They rode up to Tunstall and stopped. The Brit stared up at them defiantly.

"Deputy," he said, "do you have some reason to be on my land?"

"We're here for those horses, Mr. Tunstall."

Tunstall looked confused.

"My horses?"

"They're not your horses," Morton said, loudly. It didn't matter, though. The only witnesses were men riding with him.

"What do you mean?" Tunstall said. "They are my horses."

"No, they're not," Morton said. "Start with that one." He pointed to Tunstall's saddle horse.

As one of the men moved toward the horse, Tunstall put out a hand and said, "That's my—"

"He's goin' for the rifle!" a man shouted.

They began firing, the first shot fired by Tom Hill. Tunstall and his horse both went down in a hail of lead. Tom Hill dismounted, walked to the body and fired one round from his rifle into Tunstall's head.

TWENTY-SIX

Clint woke to pounding on his door.

"What?" Fiona asked, lying naked beside him. "Who is it?"

"I don't know," Clint said, putting his left hand on her hip and drawing his gun from the holster on the bedpost with the right, "but I'm going to find out."

He padded naked to the door, his gun more important than his clothes.

"Who is it?"

"Johnny Boggs, Clint. Open up!"

"Johnny?" Clint unlocked his door and opened it just enough for him to be able to look out. "What the hell—"

"Tunstall's dead."

"What?"

"Shot down early this morning at his ranch."

"By who?"

"A posse, supposedly. Some deputy nobody ever heard of. Mr. Chisum sent me to get you."

108

"Jesus," Clint said. "What does he want me to do?"

"Get out there, I guess. The body is still there. They're waiting for the sheriff."

"Who else is out there?"

"The Regulators," Boggs said.

"Billy?"

"I don't know, but the Regulators aren't letting anyone touch the body until the sheriff gets there."

"And where's Chisum?"

"He'll be out there."

"Okay," Clint said, "let me get dressed."

"I'll wait outside. Should I get your horse?"

"You could try, but he might kick your head in. He's crankier than me in the morning."

"I'll just wait, then."

Clint closed the door and walked to the bed to look for his clothes.

"What is it?' Fiona asked. "What's happened?"

"John Tunstall's been killed."

"My god!" she said, sitting up. "This county is gonna explode, Clint. Who killed him?"

"I don't know," he said, pulling on his pants, "but I'm going to take a ride out there and see what I can find out."

"Why you?" she asked.

"Just as a . . . favor to someone," he said, not wanting to mention Chisum's name.

She watched as she pulled on his shirt and his boots, and strapped on his gun. He ran his hands through his hair before putting his hat on.

"Sorry I have to run, Fi," he said.

"Go ahead," she said, "I understand. You'll let me know what happened?"

"Word will probably get around, but I'll let you know what I find out."

He left the room and found Johnny Boggs waiting outside. Together they walked to the livery stable, Boggs leading his horse behind him. He waited while Clint saddled Duke.

"Do you know any more than you're saying, Johnny?"

"I only know what we were told," Boggs said. "Tunstall was gunned down by a posse."

"Who saw it?"

"He had a few hands out there with him, but they turned and ran when they saw the posse."

"He was alone?"

"Apparently."

"Armed?"

"I don't know."

"Okay," Clint said, turning Duke and mounting up. "Let's go out there and find out."

When they reached the Tunstall ranch, there was a mob of people there, but the Regulators had formed a circle around Tunstall's body and would not let anyone near it.

Clint and Boggs reined their horses in, found Chisum and walked over to him. He turned and saw Clint, and moved to intercept.

"What do you know?" Clint asked.

"Tunstall was gunned down by a posse, led by some deputy named Morton."

"I don't know a deputy named Morton," Boggs said.

"Nobody does. We're waiting for Brady to come and identify him."

"Where is he?" Clint asked.

"Over there."

Clint looked at a group of men standing with their horses about fifty yards away. One of them was wearing a badge.

"And the Regulators?"

"They won't let anyone near Tunstall's body."

"Where's McSween?" Clint asked.

"On his way, supposedly," Chisum said. "He'll be able

to control the Regulators. They want to shoot it out with the posse."

"What's stopping them?"

"Me, I think," Chisum said, 'but I don't know how much longer I can keep them at bay. McSween better get here quick."

Clint looked over at the group of young men who were surrounding the body of their employer.

"Where's Bonney?" Clint asked.

"I don't know," Chisum said. "I'm afraid he may have gone after Dolan."

"If he kills him," Clint said, "he'll be in a hell of a lot of trouble."

"I think," Chisum said, "we all will."

"Look," Boggs said.

Chisum and Clint looked at the Regulators, who had all drawn their guns. Then they looked at the posse, who also had their guns in their hands. The man wearing the badge looked panicky.

"We're seconds away from a massacre," Chisum said.

"You have to stop them, John," Clint said.

"I don't think I can, Clint," Chisum said. "I should have brought my men."

"Johnny?" Clint said.

"Yep?"

"Remember all that talk about backing me?"

"I do."

"I think now's the time."

"Let's do it."

TWENTY-SEVEN

Clint moved and Boggs followed. Before long they were standing between the two opposing groups of men, who were all brandishing their guns. Clint recognized only one man, Charlie Bowdre.

"Is Bowdre leading them in Billy's absence?"

"I don't think anyone leads them in Billy's absence," Boggs said.

"That's good," Clint said, "that should work for us."

"I hope."

Clint turned to face the Regulators while Boggs faced the posse.

They stood back to back.

"You!" Bowdre said.

"You know who I am?" Clint asked. It sounded melodramatic, even to him.

"I know," Henry Brown said. "You're The Gunsmith."

"That's right."

The other Regulators exchanged glances. Clint didn't

know what was going on behind him, but Boggs could see that the name had an effect on the posse, as well. The man with the badge held his hands out to stop the others behind him.

"Now, we're all going to calm down and wait for the sheriff to get here," Clint said.

"The sheriff works for Dolan," Bowdre said. "He's gonna back this phony posse. They gunned Mr. Tunstall down in cold blood."

"Why don't we wait for the sheriff to get here and hear what he has to say?" Clint asked. "It's better than killing each other right here."

"They have to pay," Brown said, pointing to the posse.

"I'll kill the first man who fires his weapon," Clint said. "On either side."

Suddenly emboldened, Morton shouted, "You ain't even facin' us!"

"You want to try him?" Boggs asked. "Try The Gunsmith, Deputy? Who wants to go first, huh?"

"That's Boggs," Tom Hill said to Morton. "Johnny Boggs. He's pretty good with a gun."

"I'll back The Gunsmith's play," Boggs said, aloud.

"All I'm asking is that you all put up your guns until the law gets here."

"The law is in Dolan's pocket," Bowdre said.

"If that's true," Clint said, "then Mr. Chisum will call for some federal law to come in and handle things. A U.S. marshal will be here in two days."

All eyes went to Chisum, who stepped up.

"I'll send a telegram, and a marshal will here in two days," he said. "Or we can have a town marshal appointed."

"Who?" Bowdre asked.

"Somebody who is not in anyone's pocket," Chisum said. "Someone who will do what has to be done."

"Him?" Bowdre asked, pointing at Clint. "How do we know he don't work for Dolan?"

"Because he works for me," Chisum said, letting the cat out of the bag. "I asked Mr. Adams to come to Lincoln and keep a lid on things."

Henry Brown pointed to Tunstall's body.

"You call this keepin' a lid?"

"No," Chisum said, 'it's not. What happened to John Tunstall is a damned shame, and if this posse was not duly appointed then they will pay."

"Getting yourselves killed will not bring Tunstall back," Clint said. "And where's Billy Bonney? Why isn't he here?"

"Billy went—" Bowdre started, then stopped.

"If he went after Dolan, he's in the wrong, Charlie," Chisum said. "If he kills him, Billy will be the one who gets arrested."

Bowdre looked at Brown, who shook his head, but he did holster his gun.

"We'll put up our guns if they will," Bowdre said.

"Put 'em up, boys," Boggs said to the posse. "Now!"

Chisum thought he could hear the tension in his ears, like a ringing. He expected the air to be filled with the sounds of gunshots and with flying lead, but suddenly Morton slid his gun into his holster and the rest of the posse followed. Then Bowdre did the same, followed by the Regulators. The cattleman was sure that, had Clint Adams not put himself between the two factions, the ground would have been littered with many more dead men.

"Now let's just relax, and wait," Clint said, remaining where he was, his back to Johnny Boggs.

TWENTY-EIGHT

The tableau continued for almost another half an hour before the sound of an approaching horse could be heard. Nothing louder than a cough was uttered until Sheriff Brady rode into view. Chisum walked over to meet the lawman.

"You've got a lot of explaining to do, Brady," he said.

Brady dismounted and said, "What are you talkin' about?"

"Are these your men?" Chisum asked, indicating the posse.

"W-What if they are?"

"They gunned down John Tunstall."

Brady looked over to where Tunstall's body was surrounded by his Regulators.

"Was bound to happen sometime," he said.

"That's your answer?" Chisum asked. "Is that man Morton your deputy, or is he not?"

Brady had to decide who he was more afraid of, Chisum who was right there, or Dolan who was back in town.

"Let me talk to them," Brady said. "I'll find out what happened here."

"Go ahead."

As Brady approached the posse, he saw Clint standing between them and the Regulators. Clint turned his back to Tunstall's men and stood side by side with Johnny Boggs. It looked for all the world like Clint and Boggs had suddenly sided with the Regulators.

Brady approached the man wearing the deputy's badge, who he had never met before, but who he also knew worked for J. J. Dolan.

"What the hell happened?" he asked.

"He went for his rifle," Morton said. "He fired one shot and we opened fire."

Before anyone else had arrived, Tom Hill had removed Tunstall's rifle from its scabbard and fired a shot into the air. Then he laid the rifle down by Tunstall's body.

"That better be what happened," Brady said, his tone low and tense.

"It is," Hill said.

Brady nodded, then turned to walk to Chisum.

"Tunstall fired first, according to my man."

"Then he is your deputy?"

"Morton? Of course he is."

"And he claims Tunstall fired first?"

"That's right."

"That's hogwash."

"Disperse your men, Mr. Chisum, or I'll have to place all of them under arrest."

"They're not my men," Chisum said, "but let me talk to them."

"Go ahead," Brady said. "And what's Adams doin' here? He's got no right—"

"He works for me," Chisum said, and that shut Brady up.

Chisum walked first to Clint and Boggs.

"The posse claims Tunstall fired first," he said.

"Who can say he didn't?" Clint asked.

Chisum made a face. "Nobody. His men all scattered. I'm gonna try to talk to Bowdre and the others. Come with me."

He turned and walked toward the Regulators, followed by Clint and Boggs. The posse stood down and backed away, satisfied for the moment that the sheriff was handling things.

"Mr. Chisum," Bowdre said.

"Charlie, you and your boys need to stand down. We'll take Tunstall's body up to his house."

"Billy ain't gonna like this, Mr. Chisum," Bowdre said.

"Billy's not here, Charlie. You, or Henry, or somebody among you is gonna have to make a decision here."

Bowdre turned and looked at Henry Brown, and then he and Brown exchanged looks with some of the others.

"We've got to get Tunstall buried, Charlie," Chisum said. "Then we'll go to town and talk to McSween. He's a lawyer, and he'll know the right thing to do."

"Mr. Tunstall wouldn't have fired first, Mr. Chisum," Henry Brown said. "He just wouldn't've."

"Come on boys," Chisum said. "Make a decision. Do we move Mr. Tunstall's body or leave him lying there?"

They looked around at each other again, and then one of them called out, "We'll do whatever you say, Mr. Chisum."

"Good lads," Chisum said. He turned to Clint and Boggs. "Johnny, stay with me. Clint, why don't you go to town and find McSween? Maybe he can send some telegrams to try to get some outside law in here before Lincoln explodes completely."

"All right," Clint said.

"You and Johnny did a good job."

"It's nice to have somebody at my back," Clint said.

"Likewise," Johnny said. "I'm glad we didn't have to kill anybody, though."

"Clint, tell McSween to find Billy and keep him from doing something stupid."

"I'll tell him."

Chisum turned and said, "Okay, boys, let's pick up your boss and take him to the house."

Behind them they heard Brady telling the posse to mount up and return to their homes.

"I'll see you later," Clint said, nudging Boggs.

"What do you think happened here, Clint?"

"I'll tell you what I think," Clint said. "I think Tunstall would have been a fool to draw down on a posse. I think he was murdered."

TWENTY-NINE

When Clint got back to Lincoln, he went immediately to the store owned by Tunstall and McSween, but the doors were closed and locked. Billy must have gotten to McSween with the news, but then where did they go? He walked by the Big Store, which was still open and doing business. If Billy had gotten to Dolan and killed him, Clint felt sure there'd be some sign. He decided to go in and see if Dolan was there.

Riley was behind the counter, finishing up with a woman who left carrying several packages wrapped in brown paper.

"Mr. Adams, what brings you here again?" Riley asked.

"You haven't heard the news?"

"What news?"

"John Tunstall was killed this morning."

"W-what?" Riley looked genuinely shocked. "What happened?"

"He was gunned down, supposedly by a posse."

"W-why do you say 'supposedly'?"

"Because I think he was murdered."

"By who?"

"By men working for you and your partner."

Riley's eyes popped open even wider.

"I never—" he started, and then stopped.

"Maybe you didn't," Clint agreed, since the man seemed so shocked, "but what about your partner?"

"J. J.—" Riley started, and stopped again.

"Why don't we ask him, Mr. Riley? Is he in the office?"

"No," Riley said, "no, J. J. is not here."

"Are you sure?"

Riley became exasperated then and said, "I'm not lying, for Chrissake. If you don't believe me, go back and see for yourself."

"No, that won't be necessary," Clint said. "I believe you. Did Billy come by?"

"Billy?"

"Billy the Kid," Clint said. "Was he by here looking for Dolan?"

"Is he c-coming here?" Riley asked.

"Probably not," Clint said. "I think he was on his way here when he found out Tunstall was killed, but if he didn't get here by now—I think he might have talked to McSween first."

"Have you gone to their store to talk to Alex?"

"I did, but it's locked up," Clint said. "Would you happen to know where McSween lives?"

"As a matter of fact," Riley said, "I do . . ."

Following Riley's directions, Clint found his way to the McSween house. He mounted the porch and knocked on the door, which was answered by the comely Mrs. Mc-Sween.

"Mr. Adams, isn't it?" she asked. "Are you looking for Alex?"

"Yes, m'am, I am."

"I'm afraid he's not at home."

"Do you know where he is?"

"I'm afraid not." It sounded like she was 'afraid' a lot.

"How about when he'll be back?"

"I'm—"

"—afraid not," Clint finished.

"I beg your pardon?"

"Mrs. McSween, you *should* be afraid," Clint said. "This morning your husband's partner, John Tunstall, was gunned down on his ranch."

"John . . . is dead?"

"You hadn't heard?"

"My god . . . no! Who . . . who killed him?"

"A bunch of men dressed up as a posse," Clint said. "I think Dolan had him murdered. I think your husband knows about it by now, probably from William Bonney."

"My god . . . Billy will go crazy! He worshipped Tunstall."

"Mrs. McSween . . . can I come inside?"

For a moment he thought she hadn't heard him, but then she said, "Oh, yes, of course. Please, come in."

Once he was inside, she became a gracious hostess, even though she appeared to still be in shock.

"Can I offer you something? Coffee? Tea? Something stronger, perhaps?"

"No, ma'am, I'd just like to ask you a few questions."

"A-all right. Shall we sit?"

"Why not?"

She led him to the living room, which was well and expensively furnished. They sank onto a plush sofa together, albeit at opposite ends from each other. He noticed for the first time what a truly pretty woman she was. Her hair was the color of wheat, and her eyes were a brilliant blue. Her skin was very smooth and creamy. He was suddenly aware that he was looking at another man's wife, and that man might come home any minute.

"Mrs. McSween—"

"Susan, please," she said. "Call me Susan."

"Susan, I'm concerned that William Bonney might do something rash," he said. "Do you think your husband can control him?"

"Billy? I'm sure he can—at least, I think he could. Billy was closer with John—oh, I see what you mean. You're afraid Billy will go after Mr. Dolan?"

"It's possible."

"Well, yes it's possible," she said. "You're looking for my husband to find out if he's seen Billy?"

"Yes."

"Well, I don't know what to tell you, Mr. Adams—"

"Clint," he said, "you can call me Clint."

"Clint," she said. She was wearing a dress that buttoned up to her neck and fit her very well. He could see that she was not a slender woman, but was rather buxom and full-bodied. And he could smell her from across the couch, a clean smell, possibly just her soap, but an appealing smell just the same.

He had to stop. There were plenty of women around without looking at the married ones.

"I assume you went to the store . . . ?"

"I did, and it's locked up tight."

"Well, then, I'm sure Alex will be home soon, unless . . ."

"Unless what?"

She looked as if she was sorry she'd started the comment, and was afraid to finish it.

"Unless," he went on for her, "he went out to the Tunstall ranch when he heard about the shooting."

"That's possible, isn't it?" she asked.

"Yes," he said, but it wasn't. They would have passed each other along the way.

"Susan—" he started, but they were both startled when they heard a key in the lock of the front door, and then the door opened and Alex McSween came rushing in.

THIRTY

"Susan, my god—oh, Adams." He stopped short when he saw Clint. "What are you doing here?"

"Mr. Adams told me what happened to John, Alex," Susan McSween said, standing and rushing to her husband. "I'm so sorry."

"How do you know—" McSween started to ask Clint.

"John Chisum sent Johnny Boggs to get me."

"But why? You're not—wait. I see. You're working for Chisum, right?"

"Yes, I am."

"That explains a lot," McSween said. "Why you wouldn't hire on with either side."

"Yes. McSween, did Billy come and talk to you?"

"Yes, thank god," McSween said. "He came to see me before he went after Dolan. I managed to talk him out of it."

"My god, how?" Susan asked.

"I told him I'd get someone appointed to look into

123

John's death," McSween said. "That I would not let Sheriff Brady do it."

"Can you do that?" Clint asked.

"I've done it," McSween said proudly. "Darling, could you get me a whiskey? I need a drink badly."

"Yes, of course."

She started away, then stopped and said, "Clint?"

"Yes, I'll have one, thanks," Clint said.

She left the room to fetch the drinks.

"McSween?"

"A man named Bruer, R. M. Bruer, will be sworn in tomorrow as a special constable. He will then swear out a warrant for the killers of John Tunstall. He will serve that warrant and the men will stand trial."

"There was a deputy with them."

"That's what Billy said," McSween replied, "but I happen to know that Brady never had a deputy named Morton. If he happened to have one today, it's because Dolan probably made him a deputy, not Brady."

"Can he do that?" Susan asked, hearing the comment as she reentered the room with two shot glasses of whiskey. She handed Clint one, and then her husband the other.

"Not legally."

"Who's appointing the constable?" Clint asked.

"The circuit judge, who happened to be in Carrizozo today."

McSween sipped his drink, and Clint drained his. Apparently, the lawyer was not used to whiskey.

"Why a constable, McSween—"

"Oh, for Chissake, Adams, start calling me Alex."

"All right, and you call me Clint. Why not get a federal marshal in here?"

"This was quicker," McSween said. "Tomorrow I'm going to start working on getting a marshal in here. With

Chisum's help I think we can swing that. We can't let John's murder go unpunished."

"I agree," Clint said, "but what is Billy going to be doing during all this?"

"He said he'll ride with the constable to serve the warrants."

"And where will you get the names for the warrants?"

"Billy told me that Morton and Tom Hill were out there. We'll start with them and get the rest of the names from them."

"Sounds like you've thought this out."

"I'm a lawyer," McSween said. "I'm supposed to be able to think logically. I'm afraid I lost sight of that while allowing Tunstall to take things over."

"Don't—" Susan started, but her husband stopped her.

"No, you've been right all along, Susan. I followed John too blindly, forgetting that he was only twenty-three years old."

Susan put her arms around her husband's waist, and Clint suddenly felt out of place.

"Well, it seems you've got things under control," he said. "I'll be going."

He looked around for a place to leave the glass, and Susan disengaged herself from her husband and took it.

"I'll show you out."

"We'll see each other again, Clint," McSween said, "now that I know you work for Chisum. I'll be talking to him before the day's out."

Clint nodded and followed Susan to the door.

"Thank you for coming by," she said, putting her hand on his arm. "I know you did it out of concern for us."

"Yes, well," Clint said, "I think we'd better be concerned for the whole county after today."

She opened the door for him and said, "Amen."

THIRTY-ONE

It took several days, and so it was March by the time R. M. Bruer finally showed up with his warrants and put together his posse. It took the influence of both John Chisum and Alex McSween to get the new constable to add Billy the Kid to his own posse, but finally they went out looking for the guilty parties in the murder of John Tunstall.

Clint Adams did not go with them.

"It's not my job," Clint told Johnny Boggs as they stood again at the bar in Madam Varnish's place. Clint had taken to drinking only there, or more leisurely at the Wortley, on the porch.

"Mine, neither," Boggs said, "but, of course, we didn't think of that the other day when we placed ourselves between the Regulators and the posse. What were we thinking?"

"You're too kind," Clint said. "That was all my idea and you backed me up."

126

"Well then," Boggs said, "what was I thinking."

They worked on their beers for a while and Clint said, "if the Bruer posse brings back Morton and some of the others and they confess and implicate Dolan—"

"You're a very optimistic man," Boggs said.

"What do you think is going to happen?"

"I think it's more likely Billy is going to make sure he kills Morton and probably Tom Hill—maybe more of them."

"Then Dolan gets off scot-free?"

"Not as far as Billy's concerned."

"So you still think he's going to kill Dolan?"

"I'd bet," Boggs said, "that Billy's going to kill somebody—and maybe lots of somebodys."

It was the middle of the day and there was no poker game going on. The two men briefly considered playing head to head, but decided that would be fruitless. They'd simply be passing the same money back and forth between them. And the girls were all asleep, recovering from their various night's work.

"Not much happening around here right now," Boggs finally said, "so I guess I'll go back to the ranch and do some work. If you hear anything let me know."

"And you do the same."

Both nodded, and the two men, who now considered themselves friends, went their separate ways. It was several days before Clint saw Johnny Boggs again, and the man arrived in Lincoln with a tale to tell . . .

The posse led by R. M. Bruer caught up with some of the men who killed John Tunstall, including the phony deputy William Morton. Billy the Kid wanted to kill them on the spot, but the constable guaranteed the prisoners safe passage back to Lincoln.

"They brought them first to Mr. Chisum's ranch, and then left there to come to Lincoln. They never arrived."

"They were killed?"

Boggs nodded.

"We don't have the full story, yet. McNab claims the prisoners somehow got guns and started shooting. Morton, and a man named Baker tried to escape on their horses, but Billy rode them down and killed them both."

"What does the constable say?"

"He's talked with Mr. Chisum, and Mr. McSween, but from what I heard he said it just 'got out of hand.' "

"What's going to happen to the posse?"

"From what I understand," Boggs explained, "it's still going to hunt the rest of the killers."

"Billy still with them?"

"Still with them, but I don't know what Brady's going to do about this. He's still the duly elected law in this county."

"And in Dolan's pocket."

"That may be," Boggs said, "but I have the feeling he'll swear out a warrant for Billy if he can."

"Billy's riding with a posse being led by a duly appointed constable," Clint pointed out.

"I know."

Clint frowned.

"I'm starting to think I've done all I can here, Johnny," Clint said. "I'm not a duly appointed anything, and I'm not looking to get caught up in a war that's unavoidable."

"Clint," Boggs said, "I have a feeling Mr. Chisum is going to ask you to wear a marshal's badge."

"A feeling?"

"Well . . . I know he is."

"How do you know?"

"Because he asked me if I'd wear a deputy marshal's badge."

"And what did you say?"

"I said only if you were the marshal."

"So asking me to be a marshal was your idea?"

"No, that was his idea," Bogg said. "I just said I wouldn't do it unless you did it."

"Well, I won't. I wore a badge for a while early in my life, Johnny. I didn't like it."

"Fine," Boggs said. "You can tell that to Mr. Chisum when he asks you."

"I will."

They sat there in silence for a few moments, then Clint asked, "You want a beer out here on the porch? I'll go in and get them."

"Sounds good."

THIRTY-TWO

Several days later word got around that Billy had killed another of Tunstall's murderers, a man named Roberts, but not before Roberts killed the constable, R. M. Bruer. The other members of the posse tried to make Billy the leader after that, but that wasn't Billy's style. Therefore, the posse disbanded, but Billy and some of the Regulators continued looking for the last remnants of the posse that murdered Tunstall.

Clint was surprised he didn't hear from Chisum after he spoke with Boggs that day about being the marshal, but finally Chisum did send for him. Clint got a message at the Wortley to please come to McSween's law office right there in Lincoln.

Clint flipped the messenger—a young boy—a quarter and said, "Son, do you know where Mr. McSween's office is?"

"Yes, sir."

Clint waited, then asked patiently, "Will you tell me?"

The boy smiled and said, "For another quarter."

Well, Clint thought, passing the boy another coin, at least the future of Lincoln was in good hands.

When he reached McSween's law office, he found John Chisum there with McSween.

"Gentlemen," he said.

"Have a seat, Clint," Chisum said. "We want to make you a proposition."

"Is it true what I heard about Bruer?" Clint asked, sitting.

"Yes," McSween said, "if you heard he was dead."

"That's too bad."

"He wasn't doing his job, anyway," Chisum said.

"He caught most of Tunstall's killers, didn't he?"

"And lost them," Chisum said. "He let Billy kill them."

"Billy killed all of the men they caught?"

"It doesn't matter who killed them," Chisum said, "They're dead, and they were supposed to be fairly tried. This county wanted a fair trial for Tunstall's killers."

Clint looked at McSween and saw that the man didn't seem as upset as Chisum. Maybe the lawyer didn't want a fair trial for the killers of his partner.

"Clint, we have a proposition for you."

Clint knew what it was but remained quiet.

"We want you to be the marshal of Lincoln."

"No."

Chisum looked surprised.

"Don't you want to hear our offer?"

"I don't want to wear a badge, John," Clint said. "I've done it before."

"Good, that means you're experienced."

"It's not going to happen," Clint said. "In fact, I've been thinking about leaving. I don't think there's much more that I can do."

"No, no, no, no," Chisum said. "Okay, fine, don't wear the badge, but don't leave."

"John—"

"Don't beg him, John," McSween said. "I told you we don't need a marshal."

"We'll talk about it later," Chisum said.

"That's okay," Clint said, standing up. "You can talk about it now. I have to be going."

"Clint," Chisum said, "reconsider leaving town. You did a great job that day when Tunstall was killed. You kept it from turning into a blood bath out there."

"John—"

"Just give me a chance to talk to you again," Chisum said. "I'll buy you dinner tonight. If I can't convince you to stay, I won't try to stop you from leaving tomorrow."

"I wasn't going to leave tomorrow—okay, John," Clint said, instead of trying to explain himself. "You can buy me dinner tonight, but it's got to be the best steak you can find."

"Fine," Chisum said, "we'll go to White Oaks. I'll come by the Wortley around five and we'll ride over."

"Fine," Clint said. "McSween."

"Mr. Adams."

Clint left, wondering how much money Chisum was going to throw at him later that night to get him to stay.

"I still say my idea is the best," McSween said after Clint was gone.

"You're talking about vigilantes," Chisum said. "What we need is law."

"We've got law," McSween said. "Brady's the law, and look where that's got us."

"We need law that's not being controlled by Dolan's money."

"Fine," McSween said, "between you and me we can pay Brady more than Dolan is."

"What?"

"Yes," McSween said, "we turn Brady."

"How do we trust a man like that?"

"I'll tell you how," McSween said, "you pay him enough to trust him."

"You can't buy trust."

"Come on, John," McSween said, "I would have thought that by this time in your life you'd know that you could buy anything. Aren't you trying to buy Adams?"

"That's different."

"How?" McSween demanded. "How is that different?"

Chisum stood there for a moment, stumped, then stammered, "It just is!" and stormed out.

McSween sat back in his chair. He didn't need Chisum or Clint Adams. He'd get his revenge for the death of John Tunstall on his own.

THIRTY-THREE

Clint was sorry he ever came to Lincoln, New Mexico. Sure, John Chisum was a rich, powerful man, one of the few who didn't try to throw his weight and his money around to get what he wanted, who didn't try to crush the smaller ranchers who lived around him, but lived with them in peace and harmony. John Chisum was a good man, which was the reason Clint had responded to his summons. Money had nothing to do with his coming, and would have nothing to do with his staying. Chisum was going to have to come up with a damned good reason for that!

They tied their horses off and Clint followed Chisum into the White Oaks Café.

"Best steak in the county," he assured Clint.

"Good," Clint said. "I need a good steak." But it would take more than a good steak to make him stay.

When the waiter came over, Chisum ordered two steak dinners and two beers.

"Okay," Clint said, "go ahead."

"Go ahead with what?"

"Your argument for me to stay in Lincoln County."

"Oh, that," Chisum said, with a wave of his big right hand. "Forget that."

"Forget it?"

"It's not your fight," Chisum said, "and you've already done more than your share. I'll buy you your steak and you can be on your way today, tomorrow or whenever. You've got my thanks, and I'll pay you what I owe you."

"Don't talk to me about money," Clint said. "I came because you needed help."

"And I still do, but . . . it's not fair of me to keep asking you to stay," the rancher said.

The waiter returned to the table with the two steak dinners, and the two beers.

"Dig in," Chisum said. "They cook it perfectly here, and their beef is excellent."

"How do you know that?"

Chisum smiled and said, "They buy it from me."

"John—"

"Finish eating, Clint," Chisum said. "A steak like this deserves your complete attention. We can talk more afterward."

Clint studied the man as he bent to the task of consuming his steak. He's playing me, he thought. He decided that the best way to get my help is to not ask me, to tell me that it's not fair to ask me. He's playing me, all right.

And it was working, damn it.

THIRTY-FOUR

"If I stay," Clint said, over coffee, "what do you want me to do?"

"Well—"

"I'm not wearing a badge."

"Talk to Brady."

"What?"

Chisum leaned forward.

"McSween wants me to buy Brady," Chisum said, "but I always thought Brady was a good lawman—or, at least, an honest one. I think he can be turned without the benefit of a bribe."

"You think I can talk him into not accepting any more of Dolan's money?" Clint shook his head. "Your confidence in my powers of persuasion are overwhelming, John."

"Clint," Chisum said, "you have a reputation. If you appeal to him as a lawman, as an honest man, I think he'll respond to it."

"You want me to flatter him into it?"

"Whatever it takes," Chisum said. "I think it's not so much Dolan's money as it is a fear of Dolan."

"Why should he be afraid of Dolan?"

"Maybe you can find that out, as well," Chisum said. "You asked me what I want you to do? That's it. Talk to Sheriff Brady."

Clint sat back and regarded the rancher.

"You have more money than any of these people, John," Clint said, finally. "Why don't you just hire a bunch of guns—men, not boys. Why don't you bring in enough firepower to impose your own will on these people?"

"Impose my will?" Chisum said, looking stunned. "What right have I to do that?"

"You're an odd man for a rich man, John," Clint said. "Most of the wealthy, powerful men I've ever known would never have said what you just said. They'd think their money gave them the right to impose their will."

"Well, they'd be wrong," Chisum said, "and I'd be wrong to try and do that."

Clint admired the man, there was no denying. In the end, that's what made him decide to stay.

"All right, then," he said, "while I talk to Brady, why don't you talk to McSween?"

"McSween? Why?"

"Because I think something is going on with him we don't know about," Clint said.

"What makes you say that?"

"He's too damn calm about the murder of his partner," Clint said. "You know, when you have a partner and somebody kills him, you're supposed to do something about it. What's McSween doing?"

"Acting like a civilized man."

"Talk to him, John," Clint said. "If he's as civilized as you say, maybe you can get him to give up and leave, let

Dolan have business the way he wants it, the way he had
it before Tunstall came along."

"That's asking a lot of the man," Chisum said. "Tunstall was not only his partner, but his friend, as well. He's
not just going to walk away from what they built."

"And Brady's not going to turn on Dolan just because
I say please," Clint said, "but we can both try, right?"

"All right," Chisum said, tossing his hands up, "I'll talk
to Alex, but I don't know what good it will do."

"Neither one of us will know until we try."

They left the café together.

"That was as good a steak as you said it would be,
John," Clint said, "along with the rest if the meal."

"Glad you enjoyed it."

"And you got me to stay, didn't you?"

Chisum smiled and said, "I guess I did."

"You should be a politician."

"Well," the rancher said, "that's certainly something to
think about."

THIRTY-FIVE

Since no visit to White Oaks was complete without a stop at Little Casino, Clint walked over there from the café. Chisum pleaded business at his ranch, mounted up and rode off. Clint walked Duke over and tied him off outside—not that the big gelding would ever walk away, but tying him might keep some poor soul from trying to steal him and getting killed in the process. Duke didn't take kindly to strangers trying to ride him.

Clint entered Little Casino and walked to the bar. The place was just starting to come alive, with the covers taken off the gaming tables and the customers waving their money. The girls hadn't come down yet, but they'd be along soon enough—and so would Madam Varnish.

"Beer," Clint said to the bartender.

"Comin' up."

Armed with his mug, Clint turned his back to the bar to look around. At that moment two men he recognized came in—Charlie Bowdre and Henry Brown. He hadn't seen any of the Regulators since the death of Tunstall.

Bowdre recognized Clint, nudged Brown, and the two young men walked over.

"Looking for a poker game tonight, Adams?" Bowdre asked.

"Not necessariy," Clint said. "Just stopped in for a beer after a steak at the café."

"Good steak," Brown said. "That's what we should do, Charlie."

Bowdre ignored Brown.

"Don't see your friend Boggs around."

"Neither do I."

"Where is he?"

"Where's Billy Bonney?"

"I don't know where Billy is. Why are you askin' me that?"

"Because I don't know where Boggs is any more than you know where Billy is—and you're friendlier with Billy than I am with Boggs."

Bowdre looked confused.

"Come on, Charlie," Brown said. "I'm hungry."

"I want a drink first."

"Well, I want a steak," Brown said. "I'm goin'."

Brown looked at Clint, didn't say anything else, and left.

"All alone now, Charlie," Clint said, "just you and me. What's on your mind?"

Bowdre licked his lips nervously, but his youthful bravado would not let him back down.

"The others might be impressed with you, but I ain't."

"That's fine," Clint said. "I'm not all that impressed with you either, Charlie."

"Whatayou—"

"Charlie, why don't you go and have a steak with your friend," Clint suggested. "If you stay here much longer you're going to try my patience and get hurt."

"Adams—"

Clint put his beer mug down on the bar top so quickly that Bowdre jumped.

"Go, Charlie!"

Bowdre backed away, unsure how to react. When he reached the door, he turned and went through it.

"Scared him," the bartender said.

"Embarrassed him is more like it," Clint said. "Might not have been such a good idea."

"Another beer?"

"Sure, why not?"

He was still working on the second beer when the first girl came down from upstairs—Fiona.

"Now, that's what a girl likes to see," she said, coming up to him. "Her man waiting for her."

"Is that what I am?" he asked. "Your man?"

"This week, anyway," she said, with a saucy smile.

"Fiona," he asked, "do you know William Bonney?"

"Billy? Sure, all the girls know Billy. He's a wonderful dancer. He comes to White Oaks whenever there's a dance, and he dances with all of us."

"I haven't met him," Clint said. "What's he like?"

"Billy's the sweetest boy," Fiona said.

"Do you think of him as someone who kills people?"

"I don't think about that, Clint," she said, "and none of the girls do. None of us have ever seen him do anything but have a good time, and we've never known him to be anything but polite. You'll find out when you meet him."

"When I meet him?"

"Sure. Everybody in Lincoln County meets Billy at one time or another. You'll like him. You'll see." She kissed his cheek. "I have to go to work. Will you be around tonight?"

"I don't know," he said. "I can't promise anything. I'm supposed to talk to Sheriff Brady. Does he ever come here?"

"He comes," she said, "but never to gamble or be with any of the girls."

"Is he married?"

"No," she said.

"Then why doesn't he come to see the girls?"

She shrugged. "I don't know. Maybe he's . . . religious."

"Is he?"

"I don't know," she said. "I was just . . . guessing."

"Is there anyone here who knows him real well?"

"Mmm . . . I'd ask Belle."

"She knows him?"

"She seems to know everyone," Fiona said. "If she doesn't know him real well, maybe she can tell you who does. Gotta go work. If you're around later, I'll see you."

"Okay."

She went off and he put his mug down on the bar.

"Another?" the bartender asked.

"No," Clint said. "When does Belle come down?"

The bartender took a watch from his vest, checked it and said, "Any minute now."

As if on cue Belle La Mar appeared at the top of the stairs and started down. She was ensconced in what seemed like yards of red material, and men began to yell her name as she descended to the saloon floor.

"See?" the bartender said, putting away his watch. "She's always on time."

"I see," Clint said. "Thanks."

He left the bar and started across the floor to the madam, hoping he'd be able to get through all the other men.

THIRTY-SIX

Clint had his work cut out for him. For a place that had not looked busy, when Belle appeared there seemed to suddenly be more men. As Clint got closer he realized that what the men were doing was waving money and trying to make appointments with Belle's girls. Some of them were even shouting out the names of the girls they wanted to be with.

"Be calm, boys," Madam Varnish called out at one point, "there are plenty of my girls to go around. Give me a chance to catch my breath."

As if she'd spoken some magic words, the sea of men suddenly parted and Madam Varnish started walking toward the bar. When she saw Clint she smiled and waved him over.

"You're the only man not waving money," she said.

"I think we know why."

"Yes, but," she said, lowering her voice, "don't let any

of these others find out that you're bedding one of my girls for free."

"It'll be our secret," he agreed.

"Is there something else I can do for you?" she asked.

"I'd like to ask you some questions about the sheriff."

"Brady? What about him? Do you want to know if I pay him off?"

"No, that's your business," Clint said, "but I would like to know something about him."

"Come with me, then," she said. "We'll talk in the office."

He followed her to her office, where she sat behind her desk and he took a chair across from her.

"What's on your mind?" she asked, suddenly very businesslike.

"Information," he said. "They say you know everyone in Lincoln County."

"Information costs money," she said. "One of my girls you can have for free, but information costs."

"I'll pay."

She sat back in her chair. "Then ask."

"I need to know what you know about Sheriff William Brady."

"He was a decent lawman, once," she said. "He's fallen on hard times, though, and now he goes where the money is."

"Dolan, you mean?"

"Dolan," she said, "Chisum, if he'd pay."

"Why did he fall on hard times?"

"Age, mostly," she said. "He's got a problem with getting older. Also, he's had some trouble . . . uh, performing, if you get my meaning."

"I get it," Clint said. So feeling less a man, the sheriff decided to try and change that by taking Dolan's money?

"What do you think of him, Belle?"

She shrugged and said, "Not much. He was a good lawman once."

"Do you think he could be again?"

"You put that much credit to what I say?"

"I figure you for a smart woman, Belle," Clint said. "Can't run your own business without knowing something about people."

Belle studied him for a few moments, then smiled, again looking more like Madam Varnish than the businesswoman Belle La Mar.

"I think he's made a deal with the devil himself and there ain't no goin' back," she said, "except maybe for more money."

Clint nodded, stood up and started digging in his pocket.

"How much do I owe you, Belle?"

"You keep your money, honey," she said, waving it away. "I get the feelin' you're here in Lincoln County tryin' to do somebody some good. Maybe some of it will even rub off on me."

"I don't know how much good I'm going to do, Belle," Clint said, "but I appreciate the sentiment."

"If you're gonna go out there and have a beer," she said, "make sure you pay for it. You've gone and had enough freebies for ten men already. You hear?"

"I hear, Belle," he said. "Thanks."

THIRTY-SEVEN

Dolan and Riley faced each other across the desk in the office behind their store. They had just closed up and finished counting the day's take.

"J.J., I gotta ask you something," Riley said.

"What's that, partner?"

Riley sat back in his chair studied the ex–Army man he'd aligned himself with because he thought the man might make him rich.

"This business with Tunstall," Riley said.

"Business," Dolan said. "Oh, you mean his murder?"

"That's what I mean."

"You want to know if I had anything to do with it?"

"That's what I want to know, J.J."

Dolan studied his partner for a few moments, wondering just how badly the man really did want to know the answer.

"What's the difference, John?" he finally asked. "I

mean, if I say yes what are you going to do, and if I say no what are you going to do, huh?"

"I don't understand."

"Either way we're still partners," Dolan said, "aren't we?"

"That's my point, J.J.," Riley said. "If you've done anything illegal it's going to reflect on me, too."

"Illegal?" Dolan asked. "It's a little late to worry about doing something illegal, isn't it, John?"

"I'm not talking about bending the law, Dolan," Riley said. "I'm talking about killing people."

"Well, I haven't killed anyone, have you?"

"You know what I mean," Riley said, exasperated. "You're deliberately being obtuse!"

"You have to watch those big eastern words, Riley," Dolan said. "Folks around here might think you're putting on airs."

"Dolan—"

The ex–Army officer suddenly slammed both hands down on his desk and stood up, startling his partner into silence.

"All right, then, let's talk plainly, Riley! Yes, I had Tunstall killed. And I knew that Billy the Kid would eventually track down Morton and the others and kill them so they could not implicate us."

"Us? I had nothing to do with murd—"

"We're partners, Riley," Dolan said. "What one does reflects on the others, as you pointed out earlier."

"Jesus," Riley said, putting his hands in his face.

Dolan sat back down and regarded his partner dispassionately.

"Dolan," Riley said, coming out from behind his hands, "you have to buy me out."

"Impossible."

"You have the money, I know you do."

"I have it, but that's not the point," Dolan said. "For you to get out, turn tail and run at this point would not be good, John. You'll have to wait for the time to be right and then I'll make you a fair offer."

"Fair offer?" Riley said. "You'll be buying half—"

"I'll make you a fair offer for you to get out on," Dolan said. "You'll have to . . . forfeit some value, though, in order to make a deal quickly."

Riley stared at his partner for a few moments, then his shoulders slumped and he said, "Fine. Anything to get out."

Dolan leaned forward. "Just remember, John, until we make a deal we're still partners."

"What do you me—"

"I mean keep your mouth shut, partner," Dolan said, "or instead of buying you out I'll have to make other arrangements."

"Are—are you threatening me, J.J.?"

Dolan opened a desk drawer and came out with his Army Colt, the sidearm he'd worn all through his military career.

"I could kill you now, John," Dolan said, "and dispose of the body. Would you want that?"

Riley's eyes widened.

"No!" he said. "No, no, I—I wouldn't."

"Of course you wouldn't," Dolan said. "So just keep your mouth shut until this blows over, and then we'll make our deal and you can be on your way."

"W-when do you suppose that will be, J.J.?"

"Well," Dolan said, "I suspect nothing will truly be resolved until Billy the Kid is dead."

Riley closed his eyes.

"You intend to have Billy killed?"

"Before he kills me, or us," Dolan said, "yes, of course. The question, of course, is who to get to do it?"

"The Gunsmith?"

"Perhaps," Dolan said, "with a large enough offer—larger than the one we've already made him."

"You think he can take Billy?"

"I think it would be a real interesting matchup to watch," Dolan said, "but I believe superior experience will out. That, plus Billy's natural cockiness, would work in The Gunsmith's favor, don't you think?"

"I suppose."

"Are we done here for tonight, John?"

"Yes," Riley said, rising from his seat with effort, "yes, I suppose we are."

"I'll say good night, then," Dolan said, picking up a quill. "I have some paperwork to attend to."

"Yes," Riley said, moving toward the door like a much older man, "good night, then."

As the door closed behind his soon to be ex-partner, Dolan dropped his writing implement onto the desk, sat back and made a steeple of his fingers. Still more decisions to be made, he thought—deadly decisions.

THIRTY-EIGHT

The next morning Clint left the Wortley and drove to Carrizozo to see Sheriff Brady. The lawman was at his desk when Clint walked in, and didn't look too happy to have the company.

"Adams," he said in surprise. "What can I do for you today?"

"I think we got off on the wrong foot when I first got here, Sheriff," Clint said. "I thought I'd try to remedy that."

Brady looked at him suspiciously. "How?"

"I thought I'd buy you a drink." The sheriff probably got his drinks free, but Clint thought he'd make the gesture.

"It's a little early but . . ."

"A cup of coffee, then?" Clint asked. "A piece of pie." The pie seemed to do it.

"Why not?" Brady asked, standing up. "Maybe we did get off on the wrong foot, after all."

"It's your town, so you pick the place."

They started for the door and Brady said, "I know just the spot . . ."

He took Clint to a small café that was nowhere near as good as the White Oaks. Still, the coffee was drinkable and the pie was fresh. The sheriff ordered rhubarb and Clint peach.

"I think we should talk about some things, Sheriff."

"Like what?" Brady asked around a mouthful of rhubarb.

"You, Billy the Kid, Dolan."

Brady put down his fork.

"Whataya want to talk about that for?"

"Because it's important," Clint said. "The lid is about to blow off of Lincoln County, don't you think?"

"I think it already blew," Brady said. "Tunstall's dead, and I got to bring in Billy."

"Why do you have to bring in Billy?"

"Because he killed Morton and the others."

"But Morton wasn't really a deputy, was he?"

Brady didn't answer.

"You can keep eating your pie, Sheriff," Clint said. "Believe it or not, I'm here to try to help you."

"Help me with what?"

"Help you get out from under J. J. Dolan's thumb," Clint said, "or his wallet."

"Now, look here—"

"No, you look, Brady," Clint said. "I get the feeling you were a good lawman once. What happened?"

Brady glared at Clint, then pushed the remains of the pie away from him.

"You get to be my age," he said, "you'll know what happened. I got no wife, no kids, no life. I give my life to the law, Adams. You ever wear a badge?"

"I did, for a while."

"Then you know what I mean," Brady said. "I give my

life, and for what? Bad pay, free meals? I got a right to
try to make some money for myself."

"So it's the money, then?" Clint asked. "You're not
afraid of J. J. Dolan?"

"I'm afraid of a lot of things, Adams," Brady said, can-
didly, "one of them bein' you, but I ain't afraid of Dolan."

"What about Billy?"

"Yeah," Brady said. "The Kid scares the hell out of me,
but I'm gonna do my job and bring him in." He stood up
and looked down at Clint. "That happens to be what Dolan wants, and if he throws some money my way, I'm
gonna take it."

"Sheriff—"

"Thanks for the pie," Brady said. "Glad we got back
on the right foot, huh?"

"Sheriff—" Clint started again, but the man stormed
out. Clint had succeeded in getting him angry enough to
walk out, but what was he angry about? Maybe he was
ashamed, and that's where his anger was coming from.
Maybe he'd go and think it over now.

Clint finished his pie, thinking maybe he'd accomplished something and maybe he hadn't. Only time would
tell.

Billy and the Regulators were camped out, having trailed
the last remnants of the posse that killed Tunstall.

"They're gone, Billy," Bowdre said, "and who cares?
We got the main ones."

"No, we ain't," Billy said. He hadn't smiled since the
day Tunstall died, and the look he turned on Bowdre and
the others scared them. "We ain't got the main ones.
Those would be Dolan and Brady."

"Brady? Why him?"

"He deputized that Morton, didn't he?"

"Maybe he did," Brown said, "and maybe he didn't is
the way I heard it."

"He backed him that day," Billy said. "That's good enough for me."

"So what are we gonna do?" Bowdre asked.

"What we shoulda done a long time ago," Billy said. "Now, you all listen up . . ."

INTERLUDE

THIRTY-NINE

LINCOLN COUNTY, BACK TO THE PRESENT

Clint sat on the porch of the Wortley Hotel, nursing a second beer. Going back in his mind to the Lincoln County of Billy the Kid's time, he realized he'd made a lot of mistakes, but was he repeating those mistakes now in coming back? The rumor that he was there to investigate was a persistent one, but then weren't they all? What gave this one more credence than any others?

He remembered a time when there was a rumor that Wild Bill Hickok was still alive. He investigated that one, as well, and discovered a man posing as Hickok. But Hickok had been a friend of his. He'd looked into that particular wives' tale because James Butler Hickok had been a friend of his. He'd also looked into it in order to put a stop to it. William Bonney had never been a friend of his. In fact, they'd only met that one time in their lives. What, then, brought him back here to check out this rumor?

He looked up and down the main street of Lincoln, which had not changed very much since his last visit. Neither had the Wortley Hotel, except for the addition of Tim, the clerk.

As if on cue the waiter appeared at the door and came out onto the porch.

"Another beer, Mr. Adams?"

Clint looked down at the warm remnant in his mug, then handed it to Tim and said, "An ice-cold one."

"Comin' up."

Tim went back in, then returned with a frosty mug.

"Let me ask you something, Tim," Clint said, accepting the mug.

"What's that, sir?"

"Do you believe in ghosts?"

"You've heard the rumors," Tim said.

"Yes."

"Well, actually, I don't believe in ghosts, sir," Tim said, "but then I wasn't here back then, and I didn't see a body. So I guess anything's possible, isn't it?"

"I guess so."

Clint hadn't seen a body, either. He'd gone before all of that had happened.

From where he stood he could see the courthouse, and the window from which Billy had shot and killed Deputy Bob Ollinger. But that had happened long after he'd left Lincoln County. Perhaps if he'd stayed . . . but no. There was no way he could accept any complicity for the way the events played out. He'd done what he'd had to do while he was there, and then he'd gotten out. Truly, what would have been the point of staying any longer.

It probably wouldn't have changed the way things turned out, at all . . .

PART THREE

FORTY

LINCOLN COUNTY, APRIL 1878

A month of relative inactivity went by, which once again had Clint thinking of leaving Lincoln County. Chisum, however, still felt there was a slow-moving, lit fuse somewhere, and that day in April the fuse finally reached its destination.

Sheriff Brady had hired two deputies, George Hindman and J. B. Matthews. For the entire month Brady had been carrying warrants with him, intending to serve them on Billy the Kid and take him into custody. On this day Brady and his two deputies had just walked past Tunstall's store, on their way to the courthouse, when Billy the Kid and several other Regulators stepped out from behind the store and opened fire.

Brady, Hindman and Matthews were riddled with bullets and fell to the ground, dead. The Kid and his cohorts took the time to approach the bodies and inspect them before they ran off, satisfied that Brady had paid for his complicity in the death of John Tunstall. The Kid did not seem concerned with the fact that the two deputies, only recently hired, had had nothing to do with Tunstall's death, at all.

At the time of Brady's murder Clint was in White Oaks, playing poker with Johnny Boggs and several other men. Charlie Bowdre was not there because he was with Billy. They were in the midst of a big pot when someone ran in with the news.

"Sheriff Brady's been shot down by Billy the Kid!" a man shouted.

"Is he dead?" someone asked.

"He sure is."

"Where did it happen?" Boggs called out.

"Lincoln!"

Boggs and Clint exchanged glances, and then both men nodded and said, "Cash me out."

They mounted their horses and rode hell bent for leather to Lincoln to see if the news was true. When they arrived there were still people milling about between Tunstall's store and the courthouse. One of them was Alex McSween.

"Alex!" Clint shouted.

McSween turned, saw Clint and Boggs and pushed through the crowd to get to them.

"Is it true?" Clint asked. "Brady's dead and Billy shot him?"

"Not only Brady," McSween said, "but two deputies he just hired."

"Did anyone see Billy do it?" Boggs asked.

"Billy and three or four others," McSween said. "In broad daylight, and in front of witnesses."

"Who were the others?" Clint asked.

"Nobody knows," McSween said. "You know what it's like, Clint. They saw Billy, and he's the only one they cared about." McSween shook his head. "Jesus, he's gone too far this time. Killing three lawmen! What was he thinking?"

"Revenge, I guess," Clint said. "I can see killing Brady."

"What?" Boggs asked.

"From Billy's point of view, I mean," Clint explained. "He figures the sheriff had something to do with Tunstall's death. But those two deputies, they were innocent bystanders. He's going to lose some of his local support over this, don't you think, Alex?"

"Probably," McSween said.

"What about you?" Boggs asked.

"What do you mean?"

"You still going to be behind him?"

"I'll probably be his lawyer when they arrest him, if that's what you mean," McSween said. "I feel partially responsible for Billy, after all."

"I thought it was Tunstall he swore allegiance to," Clint said. "Tunstall was the one he worshipped for some reason, right?"

"I suppose," McSween said, "but John was my partner. If Billy worked for him, he worked for me, too."

Clint looked around at the crowd. Since the only law in the county was dead, no one was dispersing them. They were standing around, shaking their heads, and Clint could tell from the conversation that Billy was already losing backers.

"Where are the bodies?' he asked.

"They were moved."

"So what's everybody looking at?" Boggs asked.

Clint offered his theory that they were there because no one was telling them not to be.

"Well, we can fix that," Boggs said.

Clint nodded. He Boggs and McSween began walking around, telling people to go home.

"What's gonna be done?" somebody asked. "You can't just kill lawmen in this county."

"A new sheriff will be appointed, I'm sure," McSween answered. "Somebody will be after Billy for this."

"They better be," someone else shouted.

"This ain't right," a third voice said.

As the crowd dispersed, Clint found himself agreeing. Of everything that had happened since he arrived in Lincoln—even considering Tunstall being gunned down—this stood out as not being right, at all.

FORTY-ONE

The murder of Sheriff William Brady shocked the whole of Lincoln County. Chisum decided to call a meeting of the foes, McSween from one side and Dolan and Riley from the other. He also asked Clint to be there, as well as Johnny Boggs.

McSween was the first to arrive, finding Chisum, Clint and Boggs on the front porch. Johnny Boggs came down the steps to have someone take care of McSween's horse. McSween ascended and joined Chisum and Clint.

"A whiskey, McSween?" Chisum asked. He had a decanter at the ready on a small table nearby.

"Don't mind if I do," McSween said. "I'm thinking I'm going to need it if I'm coming face to face with the man responsible for my partner's brutal murder."

Chisum handed McSween a glass of whiskey and then said, "I'll have to have your gun, Alex."

"My gun?"

165

"The one in the shoulder rig under your jacket," Clint said.

McSween looked at Clint, then Chisum, then heard Boggs come up the steps behind him.

"What is this?"

"Don't worry," Chisum said. "I'll be asking Dolan and Riley for their weapons, as well. We don't want any shooting while we're trying to figure this whole thing out."

"When Dolan gives up his gun," McSween said, "I'll give up mine." He didn't seem too concerned about Riley. In point of fact, neither he nor Riley were very good with a handgun, but Dolan was an ex–Army man, and so was at least well acquainted with guns.

"That sounds fair," Clint said, looking at Chisum.

"All right, then."

All four men became aware of a single approaching rider. As they watched, Chisum was the first to say, "Dolan."

"Without Riley," McSween said.

"Trouble in paradise with the partners?" Clint wondered aloud.

Boggs once again went down the stairs, this time to greet Dolan and have someone take his horse.

"Gentlemen," Dolan said, joining them on the porch. "Whiskey? I'd love one."

Chisum poured him a glass and handed it to him.

"Mr. Dolan, Mr. McSween has agreed to give up his gun when you do," Chisum said. "I think it's advisable for us to have this meeting without guns."

"Does that include Adams?" Dolan asked.

"I don't think we're in any danger of Mr. Adams shooting one of you," Chisum said.

"Well," Dolan said, "there's no danger of me shooting anyone, as I'm unarmed." To illustrate, he opened his coat. True to his word, he was not wearing a gun.

"Clint?" Chisum asked.

"He's clean," Clint said, "unless he's got a hideaway in his boot."

"Be my guest," Dolan said.

"Johnny?"

Boggs had come up the steps behind Dolan. Now he bent over and checked both of Dolan's boots.

"Nothing."

"Mr. McSween?" Chisum said.

McSween hesitated, gave Dolan a suspicious look, then removed his gun from beneath his arm and handed it to Clint.

"Where's Mr. Riley?" Chisum asked. "Is he not joining us?"

"No, I'm afraid not," Dolan said. "We decided one of us should stay at the store. I hope you don't mind."

"As long as one of you is here," Chisum said. "I assume you have the authority to speak for him?"

"Oh yes," Dolan said. "I do make most of the decisions for the business, anyway."

"Why don't we go inside, then?" Chisum asked.

"I like it out here," Dolan said. "Why not just talk here?"

Clint could see what Dolan was doing, already, trying to control the situation. Before he could say anything, though, Chisum said, "Fine. Any objection, Alex?"

"No, no," McSween said, "let's just get it over with."

Clint looked at Chisum, who did not seem happy about McSween's attitude.

"My sentiments, exactly," Dolan said. "Chisum, why don't you ask McSween about hiding Billy and his gang in his house after he killed Sheriff Brady?"

"What?" McSween asked.

Dolan smiled. "Come on, Alex. Don't tell me you're going to try to deny it?"

"Alex?" Chisum said.

McSween hesitated long enough for Clint, Chisum and Boggs to realize it was true.

"I don't have to explain," McSween said. "I'm Billy's lawyer—"

"His collaborator, you mean," Dolan said. "You could be arrested for what you did, McSween."

"By who?" McSween asked. "There's no sheriff in Lincoln County."

"That's because nobody wants the job," Dolan said, "but there will be soon."

"Gentlemen," Chisum said, "I asked you here—"

"I know why you asked us here, Chisum," Dolan said, "to make peace. How can I make peace with a man who harbors a murderer?"

"And how can I make peace with a man who had my partner murdered?" McSween demanded.

"That's preposterous!"

"You're just as much a killer as Billy!"

The two men faced off and Clint thought that if they'd had guns, shots would have been exchanged.

"You're a lawyer, McSween," Dolan said. "An officer of the court. How can you condone what Billy did?"

"Me? You hired those men to kill Tunstall—" McSween stopped short and then did something that shocked everyone on the porch. He threw the rest of his drink into Dolan's face. Clint didn't know what kind of reaction he wanted, but Dolan's response was just as surprising. He remained calm and handed Chisum his own drink.

"I think this meeting is over," he said. "Mr. Boggs? Could I have my horse?"

"Dolan, you coward—"

"Coward?" Dolan asked. "McSween, I could kill you where you stand, but I was a soldier for years and you are a lawyer. That would be murder."

Dolan turned and walked down the stairs, leaving a dumbfounded McSween behind.

"Murder?" McSween repeated, finally. "Since when did you stop at murder?" But Dolan was already riding away.

"Johnny!" McSween said. "Get my horse!"

Before McSween could turn back, Clint surreptitiously removed the shells from his gun.

"My gun, Adams!" McSween demanded.

Clint made a show of checking with Chisum first.

"Go ahead, give it to him."

Clint handed his gun over. McSween shoved it back into his holster, then turned and ran down the stairs. It was clear he was going to try to catch up to Dolan.

Boggs handed McSween his horse's reins and the lawyer mounted up and rode off. Boggs came back and rejoined Clint and Chisum on the porch.

"What's going to happen if he catches up to him?" Boggs wondered aloud.

"It doesn't matter," Clint said. "Neither one of them has ever done his own killing."

Chisum shook his head, looked at Clint and Boggs, and said, "Well, that went well."

FORTY-TWO

By June a man named George W. Peppin had accepted the appointment as sheriff of Lincoln County. The first thing he did was swear in a large number of deputies and send them all out looking for Billy the Kid.

Clint was sitting on the porch of the Wortley, once again wondering why he was still in Lincoln County. He'd been there four months now, which was about three and a half months longer than he'd intended. In fact, he'd discussed that very thing with Fiona during the night, between bouts of lovemaking.

"So why don't you leave?" she asked.

"I keep asking myself the same question."

She snuggled up close to him and asked, "Could it have anything to do with me?"

It didn't, but he said, "It could . . . a little."

She pinched him and said, "Liar. You don't have to lie to me, Clint. I know I'm not going with you when you leave here. In fact, I wouldn't want to. I'm not the kind of woman who is looking for romance in her life, anyway."

"You're not?"

"No," she said. "I'm just looking for great sex, and believe me, I'm gettin' it. I'm just wonderin' when it's gonna end, because then I have to go looking somewhere else for it—and believe me, it's not easy to find—not from miners and cowpokes."

"Well, I wish I could tell you when it was going to end," Clint said, "but I can't."

"So if it's not me, what's keepin' you here?"

He thought a moment, then said, "I guess the fact that Tunstall and Brady were both gunned down, murdered. Tunstall certainly wasn't looking for that when he came over here from England, and Brady . . . well, Brady wore a badge. He shouldn't have been gunned down that way, in the street."

"So then why don't you go after Billy yourself?"

"Billy may have killed Brady, but he had nothing to do with Tunstall's death. In fact, he killed Brady because of Tunstall. I guess I don't feel that Billy the Kid is the real problem here in Lincoln."

"Then who is?"

"McSween and Dolan, I guess," he said, "but there doesn't seem to be a way to get them together."

She slid a leg over him, reached down between them and took hold of his semi-erect penis. "I guess you're stuck here with me, then, a little longer." He was fully erect now. "My god, you're just always ready, aren't you?"

He reached down to touch her and found her wet. "Look who's talking."

He pulled her on top of him and she slid up and then down, gliding him into her. He reached for her ass cheeks, cupped them and held her that way while she rode him hard . . .

But that was last night. This morning as he sat on the porch—drinking coffee this time, not beer—he saw a man wearing a badge walking toward him. He recognized him as the new sheriff, Peppin. He knew who he was because the man had decided to make his office in Lincoln, in the courthouse, rather than in Carrizozo, where Brady's office was. Peppin wanted to stay closer to the center of the action, and that seemed to be Lincoln, especially since that was where Brady was gunned down.

"Mr. Adams?" Peppin said, stopping in front of him.

"That's right, Sheriff."

"Mind if I join you on the porch?"

"Come ahead," Clint said, "it's a public place."

Peppin, a large man in his forties, mounted the porch and perched a hip on the railing, which creaked beneath his weight.

"I guess you know by now I'm the new sheriff."

"I recognize you from the courthouse."

"I intend to put a stop to all of the shenanigans that have been going on in Lincoln County."

Shenanigans, Clint thought. Was that what he called two murders—four, including the two deputies.

"That would be a welcome change," Clint said.

"To that end I'm determined to bring in William Bonney, the one they call Billy the Kid."

"Doesn't seem to me bringing in Billy's the whole answer, Sheriff."

"Perhaps not," Peppin said, "but he did shoot down my predecessor, and that's not something that cannot be allowed to go unpunished."

"What about the murder of John Tunstall?"

"Seems to me I heard Billy the Kid himself took care of most of that group."

"Maybe," Clint said, "but the man who put them up to it is still loose."

"Well, sir, Billy the Kid has been identified, and that

man hasn't," Peppin said. "I think my immediate target is clear."

"What is it you want from me, then?"

"I'm aware of your reputation with a gun," Peppin said. "I also understand you're working for Tunstall."

"In a manner of speaking."

"Well, I'd like you to accept an appointment as deputy. I could use a man like you in my quest to bring William Bonney to justice."

"Seems to me you just swore in a whole passel of deputies," Clint said.

"I have, yes, but none of them have your abilities with a gun," Peppin said. "It appears to me I'll need a man like you to bring this killer to justice. What do you say?"

"I'm afraid I have to turn you down, Sheriff," Clint said. "I've done my time behind a badge. I'm not looking to add to it."

"Well," Peppin said, "I can't offer you very much in the way of incentive. I certainly can't pay you what Mr. Chisum is paying you."

"Excuse me, Sheriff," Clint said, "but you have no idea what Chisum is paying me, or *if* he is paying me."

Peppin took his weight off the rail and stood up.

"It certainly wasn't my intent to offend you, sir."

"I'm not offended, Sheriff," Clint said, "but I'm afraid I am turning you down."

"Well, if you change your mind I'd be grateful to hear about it."

"You'll be the first to know, Sheriff," Clint said. "I can guarantee that."

He also could have guaranteed that he wouldn't change his mind, but he didn't bother adding that as the sheriff turned and walked away.

FORTY-THREE

Alex McSween closed his ledger books and pushed them away from him. There was no doubt that since Tunstall's death the store had begun to lose money. He didn't know what he was doing wrong, but more and more of the customers that they had taken away from the Big Store were going back, and he didn't know what to do. He did not have the business acumen his partner did.

He could sell the store and go back to practicing the law full time, but he had committed himself to defending Billy if and when he came to trial, and he didn't know how his law practice would stand up to that. Even many of the people in town—and in the whole county—who were firmly behind Billy were not able to condone what the Kid had done to Brady and his two deputies. McSween knew that if he defended the Kid and got him off, that would not bode well for his practice.

He picked up his gun and slid it into his shoulder rig. He'd taken to carrying the gun all the time now, even though he wasn't sure he'd ever be able to hit anything with it. There was no telling, though, when Dolan would send some of his killers after him, and he had to be ready. He had even shown Susan how to fire a rifle, and insisted she keep one nearby in the house. He had also bought her a two-shot "ladies gun" to carry in her purse when she had to go out.

He doused the light and left the store. It was not a long walk to the McSween house, which was the largest house in town. Since Tunstall had lived on his ranch, the Englishman had insisted they build a large house in town for Alex and Susan. In the beginning Susan had loved the house, but of late she was not thrilled. Maybe it was because McSween had made the house available to Billy and any of his men who needed to hide out.

It was true that McSween had hid Billy in his house right after Billy and his boys had killed Brady and the two deputies. McSween was not proud of that fact, but he still regarded Dolan as the biggest threat to him and his wife, and he needed Billy to be free to help keep them safe. He felt sure that the moment Billy was locked up, Dolan would send some of his men after both him and Susan. He tried to tell his wife that, but she was becoming less and less thrilled with harboring killers in her house.

McSween approached the door to his home, looking around quickly before slipping the key into the door and entering.

"Alex?"

"It's me."

Susan came into view from the kitchen, holding the rifle in her hands. He could not get used the sight of his beautiful wife holding a weapon in her hands.

"I can't live like this anymore, Alex," Susan said, putting the rifle down. There was a time she would have rushed into his arms for comfort after a statement like that, but no longer, for his arms offered no such comfort for her anymore.

"Susan—"

"They're going to get us killed," Susan said. "Billy and his . . . followers, they're going to get us killed, and soon."

"The sheriff has deputies all over the county looking for Billy," he assured her. "They'll find him."

"How?" she asked. "How will they find him? Every time he needs a place to hide you let him hide here. And what if they do arrest him and lock him up? Haven't you told me time and again that without Billy around Dolan would have us both killed?"

"Susan—"

"Why don't we have him killed?" she asked.

"What?"

"Dolan," she said, "let's hire someone to kill him before he kills us. Isn't that the way things are done out here?"

"Susan . . . I'm an officer of the court. I can't . . . hire a killer."

"But you can hide one in our home?" she demanded.

"That's . . . different," he said.

"How is that different?"

"It just . . . is."

"I swear to you, Alex," she cried out, picking up the rifle again, "if you don't so something about this situation, I will!"

She turned and went back into the kitchen with her rifle, leaving him there, dumbfounded.

Exactly what could she have meant by that?

FORTY-FOUR

Clint was alone in his room at the Wortley, having taken a night off from poker at the Little Casino in White Oaks, and a night off from Fiona. He was enjoying some time to himself when there was a tentative knock on the door.

Clint Adams reacted the same way whether someone was tapping on his door or pounding on it. He removed his gun from his holster and approached the door. He stood off to the side because on two previous occasions in his life someone had tried to shoot him right through a hotel room door.

"Who is it?"

"Mr. Adams?" A woman's voice. "It's Susan Mc-Sween."

If he'd expected anyone, it would have been either Fiona or Johnny Boggs. Susan McSween was a totally unexpected visitor.

He opened the door and looked out. Susan was standing in the hall, wearing the same kind of form-hugging dress he'd seen her in last time, with a shawl over it. She was rubbing her hands together, looking up and down the hall worriedly.

"Mrs. McSween," he said. "What—"

"Please," she said, cutting him off, "please, can I come in?"

"I'm alone in my room, ma'am, and it wouldn't be right—"

"I don't care!" she hissed at him. "Please!"

He stepped back and allowed her to enter, then closed the door behind her.

She saw the gun in his hand and said, "I can't blame you for that. I carry this, myself."

She reached into her purse and took out a two-shot derringer. He hurriedly removed it from her hand. "Don't take that out unless you're going to use it." He opened her purse and shoved the gun back into it. Then he walked to the bedpost and holstered his own. He doubted she was there to shoot him.

"What can I do for you, Mrs. McSween?"

"Susan," she said, "call me Susan . . . Clint."

"All right, Susan," he said. "Does your husband know you're here this late at night?" It wasn't late—maybe eight or so—but it was late for a married woman to be in a man's hotel room.

"No, he has no idea," she said. "I slipped out the back door."

"And why did you do that?"

"To come here and talk to you—actually," she said, immediately amending the statement, "I need you to kill Billy, and then J. J. Dolan."

Clint hesitated a moment, then asked, "is that it? Just the two of them?"

"Yes," she said, "just those two."

"And that would solve all your problems?"

"Yes," she said, seeming calmer now that she had gotten that out, "it would."

"Susan," Clint said, "I think you'd better sit down."

There was a chair in the room, but Susan McSween chose to sit on the bed as she instantly obeyed.

"I know things have been hard, of late," Clint said, "but you can't just ask someone to kill someone else—"

"Why not?" she asked, cutting him short. "Isn't that the way things are done out here? I thought it was done all the time. Look at John Tunstall, and Sheriff Brady. They were shot down, weren't they?"

"Well, yes, but—"

"And I'm not asking you to kill them for free," she added. "I'm quite willing to pay you. Tell me, what is the going rate to kill a man?"

"I don't know the going rate—"

"Why not? Isn't that what you do?"

He stared at her, wondering if she intended to ever let him finish a sentence.

"Ma'am," he said, "you're going to have to shut up for a minute and let me talk."

Susan blinked, having never been told that before by a man, but then she nodded and said, "Very well."

He remained standing because he thought he probably needed to be looking down at her to keep her quiet.

"First of all, I don't know what you heard, or what your husband told you, but I don't hire out to kill people. Second, having people killed is not the answer."

"Why not?"

"Because . . . it's not. You may have heard wild stories about the West and how we kill people, but it's not the way."

"Judging from what I've seen here in Lincoln County, it certainly is." She stood up. "I suppose I'll have to find someone else to do it. I have money, you know."

She reached into her purse and he tensed for a moment,

wondering if she was going to come out with that gun. Instead, her hand came out holding a wad of money.

"Susan," he said, "put that away . . . and sit back down!"

She sat, and tucked the money away in the bag.

"I thought you'd change your mind when you saw the money," she said, smugly.

Clint studied the woman. She had the glassy eyed look of a person who was in shock. He wondered if something had happened at her home, between her and her husband, to perhaps set her off.

"Susan," he said, patiently, "I have not changed my mind. I just don't want you walking up to some man with a wad of money like that."

"Why not?" she asked. "*Somebody* will take the job."

"It's more than likely somebody would take that money away from you, and then take a lot more. You have to be careful who you talk to like this."

"Aren't you the one everyone calls The Gunsmith?"

"Yes."

"And you have a reputation."

"Yes."

"And a lot of people are afraid of you."

"I suppose—"

"And could you kill Billy the Kid if you had to?"

He stared at her, and then said, "I don't know. I've never seen the Kid handle a gun."

"But you are very good with a gun."

"Yes."

She shrugged and said, "I don't understand. Why won't you take the job? Once you've killed Billy, Dolan should be easy."

"Susan, why do you want these men killed?"

"Because if we don't kill them first," she said, "one of them will kill us. I'm sure of it."

"I thought Billy worked for your husband and Tunstall."

"He worshipped Tunstall, although God knows why. He doesn't feel that way about Alex."

"But he does work for him?"

"Yes."

"Then why would Billy kill him, or you?"

"Billy won't kill us," she said, "but he'll get us killed."

"How?"

She hesitated, then said, "Alex lets him hide in our house when he's in town."

"Well, that's no surprise," Clint said, although this was the first time he'd heard Dolan's accusation confirmed.

"They'll come for him eventually," she said. "They'll guess where he is, or find out, and they'll come for him, and we'll be killed in the crossfire."

"And Dolan?"

"Dolan will kill us once Billy is locked up. Then he'll have no competition. For him, things will be back to the way they were before John Tunstall convinced my husband to go into business with him here in Lincoln."

"Susan," Clint said, "I can appreciate you concern, I really can. But you can't go around trying to hire someone to kill Billy and Dolan. Money doesn't buy everything, you know."

He walked to the window and looked out. He could see the main street from here, and it was quiet and empty. He heard a rustling of fabric behind him and then Susan McSween said, "if you don't want money, would you take this?"

He turned and was shocked to find her standing there with her dress peeled down to her waist!

Clint shook off his surprise, approached her and pulled the dress back up to her shoulders. It wasn't easy, because her breasts were flawless—large, firm, with smooth, pale skin and big pink nipples. She was another man's wife, though. Not that he had never slept with another man's wife, but this was a man he knew. Briefly, the backs of his hands made contact with her skin, which made it even harder to back away from her.

"Susan," he said, "I'll see what I can do about this whole situation. That's why I'm staying, to see if I can have any effect. There's no need for you to try to buy a gun, or to . . . do this!"

Her face flushed with embarrassment as she buttoned up her dress.

"Go home to your husband. If you really want to get this resolved, why don't you see if you can get him to leave here with you? Go start over somewhere else, where no one is being killed."

"I've tried that," she said. "He won't leave. This is all going to come to a bad end, and there's nothing I can do about."

"Well, maybe there is something I can do," Clint said. "Just . . . go home. Don't try this with someone else, Susan. They might not be as . . . understanding."

Susan nodded, turned and walked to the door, keeping her head down, averting her eyes, feeling ashamed of what she'd done. Clint didn't know what else he could do for the woman.

She opened the door, then turned and finally looked at him with haunted blue eyes.

"Thank you, Clint . . . thank you for . . ." She didn't finish, just walked out and closed the door behind her.

Clint walked to the window and looked out, watching her walk away. The backs of his hands still burned where they had touched her skin. He told himself that she was beautiful and desirable, but so were a lot of women. Perhaps what made her so attractive was that she was unavailable—although she hadn't been so unavailable a few moments ago.

He turned away from the window and wished Fiona was there at that moment.

FORTY-FIVE

One of the men Sheriff Peppin had deputized was named Marion Turner. Turner had a force of men with him, head-quartered at Roswell. The events that would lead to a bloody battle in Lincoln began when one of Turner's men rode into Roswell with news for him.

"I saw 'em," he said to Turner.

"Saw who?" Turner asked. Of an age with Chisum, Turner had for years been on-again-off-again in the employ of the rancher. However, for reasons all his own he had recently become opposed to Chisum, and accepting an appointment as one of Peppin's deputies was his way of taking a more active roll in his opposition.

"Billy the Kid, and his men," the other deputy said. "They were heading in the direction of Chisum's spread."

They had known for weeks that the Kid had some sort of stronghold along the Rio Pecos. Now he had shown himself, probably heading for Chisum's for some supplies, or even shelter.

"Get the men," Turner said. "We're riding for Chisum's ranch!"

It took a short time to amass thirty or forty deputies, who all left Roswell at a gallop, heading for John Chisum's ranch.

Chisum was surprised to see Billy ride up onto his place with about fourteen of his men.

"There are warrants out for you, Billy," he said.

"I know that, Mr. Chisum," the youngster said. "My boys are hungry, and thirsty. Can we light and set a spell?"

"Of course you can, lad," Chisum said. "I'll have the cook set up some grub for you."

"Thank you, sir."

Chisum's cook fed the force of fifteen men in the mess, and that's where they were when one of Chisum's riders came in with news.

"Mr. Chisum," he said, dismounting on the run, "Deputy Turner's on his way here with thirty or forty men."

"He must have heard Billy was here," Chisum said.

Billy stood up and said, "We'll be on our way, Mr. Chisum. No need for us to visit our troubles upon you. We're obliged for the food and drink."

"Never mind, boy," Chisum said. "You'll not outrun that bunch, and you're badly outnumbered."

"What do we do, then?" Billy asked.

"You'll go inside the house," Chisum said. "My buildings here were built to repel Indian attacks, I guess we'll be able to stand off a posse."

"You'll shoot it out with the posse for us?" Billy asked.

"Hopefully, it won't come to that," Chisum said. "Take your men inside. I'll talk to the deputies."

"Mr. Chisum," Billy said, "Mr. Tunstall did just about the same thing, and he got killed."

"Billy, I know Marion Turner. He's a duly appointed

deputy of Sheriff Peppin's. He's not gonna shoot me down."

"But, sir—"

"Go on into the house, Billy," Chisum said. "Do what somebody tells you, for once."

Rather than bristle at the comment, as some of his men thought he might, Billy simply said. "Yes, sir."

Bowdre whispered to him urgently, "What are you doin', Billy? What if he turns us over to the posse?"

"He won't," Billy said. "I trust Mr. Chisum."

"So we all gotta trust him with our lives?"

"Ride out if you want, Charlie," Billy said. "Anybody wanna ride out with Charlie here?"

None of the other men spoke up. In fact, they looked away.

"You wanna go, Charlie?" Billy asked.

"Not alone, I don't."

"Well, then," the Kid said, "everybody into the house."

When Turner and his posse reached the ranch, they were met by Chisum and his foreman, Johnny Boggs. Boggs also knew Turner from past dealings.

"Johnny, Mr. Chisum," Turner said. "We got word that Billy the Kid was headed your way."

"Is that a fact?"

"Yes, sir, it is," Turner said. "I'd be obliged if you'd turn him over to me so that me and my men don't have to go into your house and fetch him out."

"You haven't even asked me if he's here," Chisum pointed out.

Turner leaned back in his saddle and thought a minute.

"Mr. Chisum, there's a bunch of tracks leadin' right into your place," Turner said. "Now, they coulda been made by your own men, but they're real fresh and I kinda doubt it. I think Billy is holed up in your house."

"If you think that," Chisum said, "then go in and get

him, but keep this in mind: My house was built to withstand Indian attacks. There are gun ports below every window. Now, you got a lot of men with you, but I'll bet . . . oh, fourteen or fifteen men inside my house would be your equal. What do you think, Marion?"

Turner looked around at his men, who suddenly found something very interesting in the sky. The decision was his and his alone.

"Mr. Chisum," he said, finally, "if I try to take Billy, will you and your men interfere?"

"If we did," Chisum said, "it would be you who was outnumbered, wouldn't it, Marion? You've worked here on and off. You know how many men I have."

Turner just stared at Chisum, trying to figure out exactly what the man's answer was.

"But no, Deputy, we wouldn't interfere. After all, you probably have warrants, don't you?"

"I do."

"Well, there you go," Chisum said. "We wouldn't think of trying to stop you from serving legal warrants . . . would we, Johnny?"

"Not at all, Mr. Chisum," Boggs said, "but you know what?"

"What's that, Johnny?" Chisum asked.

"If Billy and his men are in your house—and I'm not saying if they are or aren't—I bet they wouldn't need any help to hold these boys off. I mean, that house is solid. It'll stand up to a lot of lead, I bet. And I wouldn't want to be part of the group that tried to storm it, no sir."

"Good point, Johnny," Chisum said, "real good point. Well, we best step aside, then."

Both Chisum and his foreman moved out of the posse's way.

"Go ahead, Deputy," Chisum said, "serve your warrants."

The play was squarely on Turner's head, and lives of

some fifty or sixty men—counting both sides—were in his hands. But more importantly to Turner, his life was one of them.

"I think we'll back off and watch a spell," Turner said then.

"Up to you, Deputy," Chisum said. "Entirely up to you."

"Yeah," Turner said, "I think that's what we'll do."

Chisum and Boggs watched as the posse withdrew to a distance from which they could still see the house.

Chisum looked at Boggs and blew a breath out that he'd been holding for some time.

FORTY-SIX

It was decided—by Chisum, with Billy agreeing to it—
that Billy and his men would not leave the Chisum house
as long as Turner and his posse were outside.

"That could take weeks!" Charlie Bowdre complained,
after Chisum and Boggs left the house to check on the
posse again.

"I can think of worse places to be holed up," Henry
Brown said.

"It's not gonna be weeks," Billy said. "Mr. Chisum
knows Turner better than I do, and even I know he'll get
impatient and back off, hoping that we make a move."

"And will we?" Bowdre asked.

"We will," Billy said, "but when the time is right."

"And who says when the time is right?" Bowdre asked.
"Us or Chisum?"

Billy gave Bowdre a hard stare and said, "Me, Charlie.
You got a problem with that?"

"No, Billy," Bowdre said, "I got no problem with that."

"Good . . . and I want you fellas to take it easy on Mr. Chisum's furniture. Charlie, get your feet down!"

"We're gonna do what?" one of the deputies asked Marion Turner.

"We're gonna withdraw," Turner said, "except for one man who's gonna keep watch."

"But . . . why?" the other man asked. Some of the other deputies gathered around to hear the reason, too.

"Because Bonney and Chisum both think they know me," Turner said, "and it's me who knows them."

"I don't get it," the first man, whose name was Doug Sharp, said. "Why leave a man on watch when we know he's in there?" Sharp took off his hat and scratched in confusion at the tight growth of gray hair on his head.

"Billy and Chisum think I'm gonna get lazy and pull back," Turner said. "They're thinkin' Billy will pull out when I do that."

"But that is what you're gonna do . . . right?" the second man asked. His name was Ken Sweetzer, and he was just as confused as Doug Sharp was.

"We're all pullin' back but you, Ken," Turner said.

"And what do I do?"

"Wait for Billy and his men to pull out."

"But . . . they'll get away."

"Not if I'm right about where they'll be goin'."

"And where's that?"

"To Lincoln."

"Why would they go to Lincoln?" Sweetzer asked. "Everybody there knows Billy, and will be lookin' for him."

"That's why he'll go there," Turner said. "Because he doesn't think anybody will be lookin' for him where he'll go—but I will. And do you know where?"

"Where?" Sharp asked.

"McSween's house," Turner said. "It's the only place

big enough, and it's well built. They'll think they can hold out there, but we'll get 'em out."

"Aren't we jumpin' the gun here?" Sweetzer asked. "We don't even know for sure he'll go there."

"You just come and get the rest of us when they pull out," Turner said. "They'll go there."

Now it was Sweetzer's turn to scratch his head, only his hair was thick and black. "I hope you're right, Deputy."

"Don't worry, Ken," Turner said. "I'm right."

Boggs came into the house several hours later with the news.

"Withdrew to where?" Chisum asked.

"They're gone, near as I can tell," Johnny Boggs said. "Except for one man."

"I don't like it," Chisum said. "Turner's up to something."

"Time for us to go," Billy announced to his men.

"Billy—"

"Sorry, Mr. Chisum," Billy said. "Turner might be plannin' something, but it's time for us to be movin'. Thanks for your hospitality."

"Billy . . . good luck."

"Yes, sir," Billy said, "but I don't think I'm the one who's gonna be needin' the luck."

Billy and his men had started for the back door when it suddenly occurred to Chisum what the young man might be planning to do.

"Billy," he said, "you're not going to Lincoln, are you?"

"Better you don't know where we're goin', Mr. Chisum," Billy said. "That way you don't gotta lie to the law when they ask."

He followed the last of his boys out the back door.

"Where do you think he's going, Boss?" Boggs asked.

"Lincoln is where he's going," Chisum said. "I think he's finally decided to go after Dolan."

"About time, I say," Boggs commented.

"He'll get himself and his men killed," Chisum said. "Sheriff Peppin is in Lincoln."

"Billy hasn't had any difficulty with lawmen up to now," Boggs pointed out.

"Maybe not," Chisum said, "but this one might be waiting for him."

Ken Sweetzer rode into the posse's camp and dismounted.

"So?" Turner asked him.

"It's just like you said," Sweetzer answered. "Billy and his men pulled out a little while ago and headed in the direction of Lincoln.

"Get the men mounted," Turner said. "We're goin' to Lincoln to get that little killer!"

FORTY-SEVEN

Something was in the air. Clint Adams could feel it from where he was sitting on the porch of the Wortley. Maybe it was because he was anxious to move on, and he was just hoping that something was going to happen, but no . . . he definitely felt something in the air.

He was still sitting on that porch when Billy the Kid and his boys came riding into Lincoln bold as brass. They rode past the courthouse to show their utter disdain for Sheriff Peppin, and Clint got his first real look at Billy the Kid. He looked like a scrawny kid atop his gray horse, not a dangerous killer at all. But Clint had known killers who looked like saints, and Billy the Kid was no saint.

Clint stood up and stepped into the street to see where the Kid was leading his Regulators. They rode past both stores, reined their horses in in front of Alex McSween's house and dismounted. Clint knew that the McSween house—almost a mansion—was the sturdiest building in

Lincoln. Apparently, the Kid had chosen to make a stand there.

Clint wondered how Alex and Susan McSween were going to feel about his decision.

"Billy!" Susan McSween said when she opened the door. She looked past him and saw about fourteen other young men. "W-what are you doing here?"

"I'm sorry, ma'am," Billy said, "but we have to come in." He pushed her back as gently as he could, without touching her, and the others followed him in. "Is your husband here?"

"N-no, he's at the store. W-what's going on?"

"Close the door, Henry!" Billy shouted to Henry Brown. "Mrs. McSween, you have to go and get your husband. We need to talk to him right away."

"Billy . . . you can't keep coming here to hide out," Susan said, "you can't. My husband has been more than fair with you—"

"Yes, ma'am," Billy said, "I know that, and we appreciate it, but right now you need to go and get him. The sooner we talk to him, the sooner we'll be gone."

Susan glared at Billy, feeling totally helpless, then said, "Oh, very well." She glared at the other men, then pushed past them and went out the front door.

"Sheriff!"

Peppin looked up at the man who'd stuck his head in his office and called his name. He didn't know his name, but had seen him around the courthouse.

"What is it?"

"You better come quick."

"Wha—"

"Billy just rode in, with a bunch of others."

"Bonney? He's in town now?"

"Yes, sir."

"Good God!" Peppin said. He grabbed his hat and gun and stormed out of the office.

Clint saw Susan McSween walking purposefully up the street until she reached her husband's store, and then she rushed in. Moments later she came out, following her husband, trying to keep up with his longer strides.

From the other end of the street there was the sound of horses, and when he looked he saw a group of men—forty, maybe fifty—riding down the street. The light glinted off the badge on the chest of one of them.

When they reached the courthouse, the door opened and Sheriff Peppin came rushing out. He stopped when he saw the posse and began to talk to the other man with the badge.

The stage was set—for a catastrophe.

FORTY-EIGHT

Clint crossed the street to confront the sheriff and his deputies in front of the courthouse.

"What do you want, Mr. Adams?" Peppin asked.

"Billy's in the McSween house," Clint said. "What do you plan to do?"

"That's none of your business, I'm afraid," the lawman said. "You had your chance to be part of this posse."

"This posse?" Clint repeated, looking at the motley band. "I'm glad I turned it down."

"Look here—" Turner started.

"You look," Clint said, cutting the man off, "Susan McSween is in that house. I want to know what you're planning to do."

"We're gonna get them out of that house," Turner said, "one way or another." He ignored Clint then and addressed himself to the sheriff. "We tracked Billy and his men here, Sheriff. This is my show to call."

"I'll allow that," Peppin said. "You can count on me to back you."

"Thank you."

"Sheriff—"

"I'll have to ask you not to interfere, Adams," Peppin said, "or I might have to lock you up."

Clint stared at the lawman and decided not to push it. He could help more out of jail than in—the question was, help who?

When McSween entered his house with his wife following him, Billy said, "You shoulda left your wife behind, Mr. McSween. This is not gonna be anyplace for a woman."

"Billy, what do you plan to do?"

"We're gonna make a stand here, Mr. McSween," Billy said. "This place is like a fortress. We can stand them off here forever."

"You don't have forever, Billy. You should give up now, before things get out of hand."

"Mr. McSween," Billy said, "Mr. Tunstall's dead, and I killed three lawman. I think things are already out of hand, don't you?"

"Billy," McSween said, "you've got to get out of my house before—"

Before McSween could finish, there was a voice from outside.

"Billy?" a man called. "Billy Bonney? This is Deputy Sheriff Marion Turner. I have Sheriff Peppin out here with me as well as forty men. The house is surrounded. I'm advising you to come out with all your men, and your hands in the air."

"Billy, give up."

Billy looked at McSween and said, "They're not gonna take be alive, Mr. McSween."

"Hello the house," Turner called. "I have warrants out

here for the arrest of W. H. Bonney and others in the house. I advise you to come out."

"The windows," Billy said, and quickly men like Charlie Bowdre, Henry Brown, Dave Rudabaugh and Tom O. Foliard went to the windows with their guns ready.

"Turner," Billy shouted, "we have warrants, too, and we'll serve them with hot lead."

Billy started shooting, and the rest of his men followed. Returning fire came from outside. Windows were broken, and fixtures inside the house were shattered, but very little damage was done to the structure of the house itself.

"Yes," Billy said, when the shooting stopped, "we can hold out here for a long time."

Clint watched as the posse returned the fire that was coming from inside the house. He saw the lead slam into the wall of the house with little effect, but knew that glass and fragments had to be flying inside. He hoped Susan McSween was crouched down behind a big piece of furniture. He felt badly that he had assured her he would try to do something to avoid all this, and he had not gotten it done. Now, if she ended up dead . . .

The standoff continued most of the day and into the night. By morning a few stray shots woke everyone up, including Clint, who had been dosing on the Wortley porch. He'd decided not to sleep in his room, in case anything happened during the night.

He heard a door open and turned to see Sam Wortley coming toward him carrying a cup of steaming coffee.

"Thought you could use this."

"Thanks," Clint said, accepting the mug, "you're a lifesaver."

"How long do you think this will go on?" Wortley asked, looking down the street. He couldn't really see the

McSween house, but a crowd was already beginning to gather to watch the day's events.

"I don't know," Clint said. "I guess it depends on how badly the law wants to get Billy out."

"What do you mean?"

"I mean that house can stand up to a ton of lead, but if they called in the military . . ."

"You mean . . . like a cannon?"

Clint just shrugged.

"Jesus, they could bring the whole house down!"

"Yes, they could," Clint said.

FORTY-NINE

Clint approached Sheriff Peppin later that day and said, "I want to go in."

Peppin turned his attention away from the house and looked at Clint.

"You want to go in . . . where?"

"Into the house. I think I can talk Billy into giving up."

"Do you know him?"

"We've never met."

"What makes you think he'll listen to you?"

Clint shrugged and said, "Where's the harm? At the very least I can bring Mrs. McSween out. She doesn't belong in there. Neither does McSween."

"He chose sides a long time ago," Peppin said, "but you can go in and get the woman—that is, if they don't kill you first."

Clint removed his gun from his holster, handed it to the lawman and said, "Why don't we find out?"

"What's going on?" Turner asked, noticing Clint for the first time.

"Adams is going to try and talk Billy out."

"What? I didn't okay that."

"I did."

"I thought this operation was mine to run," Turner snapped.

"It is," Peppin said, "but if it can end without bloodshed, why not take the chance?"

"No bloodshed?" Turner asked. "Billy will shoot Adams down just to be able to say he did."

"I think the decision in up to Adams," Peppin said.

"I'm going in," Clint stated firmly.

"Fine," Turner said, "it'll be just another murder to charge Billy the Kid with."

Peppin looked at Clint and nodded. "Go ahead."

"Hello the house!"

"Who's that?" Billy asked, looking at McSween.

The lawyer came to the window and looked out.

"That's Clint Adams."

"The Gunsmith?" Billy asked. "I heard he was here, but our paths haven't crossed."

"They have now," McSween said.

"McSween? I want to come in and talk to Billy!"

McSween looked at Billy, who nodded and said, "Why not?"

"I'm unarmed."

"Even better," Billy said, and pointed his gun at Clint through the window. "Tell him to come ahead."

FIFTY

Clint started toward the house with his hands held away from his body. He didn't think Billy would shoot an unarmed man, but he tensed just the same.

As he reached the front porch, the door opened and McSween appeared.

"Whatever happens," the lawyer said as Clint reached him, "you have to take my wife out of here."

"That was my plan."

Clint entered the house and McSween closed the door. Immediately ten guns were trained on Clint.

"Billy?" Clint said, looking at the Kid.

"You know me?"

"Only by sight," Clint said. "From descriptions."

"Well," Billy said, "I've heard of you, but I ain't never seen you. So you're The Gunsmith, huh?"

"That's right."

"Bet you ain't too comfortable with that empty holster."

"It does feel kind of . . . light."

"Yeah," Billy said, holding his gun loosely in his hand, "I can sympathize."

The two men stared at each other for a few moments, then Billy holstered his gun. The other men, however, covered him.

"Okay, so why'd you wanna come in here?"

"Well, for one thing I think Mrs. McSween should be allowed out of the house before she gets hurt."

Susan McSween was standing behind the men with the guns, looking harried.

"I'm not leaving," she said.

Billy turned and looked at her, then back at Clint. "I don't see any reason why she can't leave."

"Except that I don't want to."

"You're leaving, Susan," McSween said to his wife.

"Not without you."

"No," he said, "I'm staying with Billy."

"You can take Mrs. McSween," Billy said to Clint. "What else?"

"Well," Clint said, "I was kind of hoping I could talk you into giving yourself up. There's forty men out there, and there's probably going to be some help coming from Fort Sumner."

"We're pretty secure in here," Billy said. "We got ammunition, food and water."

"What good is this doing, Billy?" Clint asked. "Hasn't there been enough killing?"

"Not quite," Billy said, obviously referring to Dolan.

"What about your men?"

Billy looked around at them, and nobody spoke.

"Guess not," the Kid said. "What next?"

"Billy—"

"I appreciate you coming in here, Mr. Adams," Billy said, "especially without your gun. That took guts."

"Look—"

"But we're not leaving until we're ready. I'm sorry."

The Kid looked perfectly calm, no trace of madness in his eyes. He seemed in complete control of himself.

"Billy," Clint said, "I hope you survive to dance again."

"Yeah," the Kid said, "so do I. Take Mrs. McSween and go."

McSween walked to his wife and put his arms around her. She clung to him.

"If you get killed I'll never forgive you," she said.

"I'll try not to. Now go with Mr. Adams."

She walked past the men with the guns and Clint reached out for her hand. McSween started for the door ahead of them.

"Mr. Adams," Billy said.

"Yes?"

"What's it like to be as famous as The Gunsmith?"

"It's not something I'd recommend to anyone, Billy."

"Well," Billy said, "I'm gonna be as famous as you someday—maybe more famous."

"Would that be alive," Clint asked, "or dead?"

Clint left the house with Susan McSween and sent her to the Wortley Hotel.

"Well?" Peppin asked.

"He's not coming out," Clint said. "None of them are."

"You're lucky he didn't kill you."

"I guess."

"We won't be needing your help anymore after this, Mr. Adams," Turner said.

"Have you called for military help?"

"I've sent someone to Fort Sumner," Peppin said. "The military will get him out of there."

"I'll get him out," Turner said. "I swear."

Clint took hold of the sheriff's arm and waked him out of Turner's earshot.

"Watch out for him," he said. "Right now I think he's more dangerous than Billy."

"I'll keep that in mind, Mr. Adams," Peppin said, removing his arm from Clint's grasp. "For now I'll ask you to withdraw."

FIFTY-ONE

On Day Two John Chisum rode in to try and talk Billy out, but to no avail. He and Boggs ended up on the Wortley porch with Clint.

"I'm sorry I got you into this, Clint," Chisum said. "You've wasted months here only to watch it come to this."

"I could have left anytime, John," Clint said. "It was my choice to stay."

"Poor Billy," Boggs said.

"Poor Billy?" Chisum said, giving his foreman an odd look. "I tried to help him all I could, Johnny. He killed three lawmen, for Chrissake!"

"I just mean this won't end until he's dead, that's all," Boggs said.

"It ends for me now!" Chisum said, standing up. "I'm done with him. I'll see you back the ranch."

Chisum stalked off.

"Think he means it?" Clint asked.

205

"He means it all right," Boggs said. "When he makes up his mind . . . Well, Billy's already dead to him.'

"He was right, then."

"About what?"

"I have wasted my time here."

Boggs stayed another hour, then he went back to the Chisum ranch.

The military did not arrive until Day Three, and then they did they were not from Fort Sumner, but from Fort Stanton. Lieutenant Colonel Dudley of the ninth Cavalry arrived with one company of infantry and one of artillery.

Dudley's idea was to put one of his guns in a depression on the street, right between the two factions. He swore to use it on the first to fire, but he never did. The Army's presence was all show, as they did nothing to try to get Billy out of the house, or to disperse the posse.

They were useless.

Susan McSween sat with Clint on the porch of the Wortley on the fourth day, listening to the sporadic gunfire.

"It can't go on like this," she said.

"It won't," Clint assured her. "Something's going to happen, and it'll happen soon."

"You told me this wouldn't happen," she reminded him.

"I was wrong."

"Why should I believe you now?"

"You shouldn't."

She frowned and said, "But I do."

Day Four went by uneventfully, a few shots fired when somebody got nervous, or someone saw a head pop up as a target. Most of the citizens of Lincoln had even gotten bored and were now staying off the streets.

Clint walked down to the scene every so often, and when he saw that nothing was happening, he walked back to the hotel. Susan McSween had not come out of her room at all that day. Maybe she could feel tension in the air the way Clint could.

An explosion was coming, and he wasn't sure why he was staying around to see it.

Finally, on Day Five, it came.

Clint walked over to the McSween store and found it locked up. He'd been curious if clerks had been keeping it open. As he peered through the windows, he realized how bored he had become. He turned to walk back to the hotel, but someone shouted something from the end of the street and he wondered why it hadn't happened before this.

"The house is on fire!" a man shouted. "The McSween house in on fire!"

FIFTY-TWO

Clint ran down the street. He saw the smoke first, and when he reached the house he saw the flames. The front of the house was burning, flames coming out the windows.

"Who did that?" he asked Peppin.

I don't know," the sheriff answered, "but it should bring them out now!"

"Or burn them all to death," Clint said, angrily.

The flames were so white hot that he knew someone had poured something on the house before lighting it. There was no chance in hell that this fire was accidental.

"Get ready, men!" Marion Turner shouted. "They should be coming out any minute, and when they do, open fire."

"Wait!" Clint shouted. "Let them surrender."

"They had their chance to surrender," Turner said. He turned and told some of his men to be sure the back was covered. "The Rio Bonito's only fifty feet from the back of the house."

That would be the smart thing to do, Clint realized. Head for the river.

Inside the house there was panic.

"Whata we do?" Henry Brown shouted. The flames were hot, and they were loud. Billy was surprised at how loud the crackling of the flames was.

"We get out," Billy said, "any way we can! Move. It's every man for himself!"

The fire surprised Billy. He hadn't thought of this, and he didn't know how to react except to get out and run. Going out the front door, however, into most of the guns, was not an option for him. Unfortunately, Alex McSween did not think that quickly.

Billy saw McSween head for the front door, and before he could call out to him, the lawyer was out the door, several men running out behind him. Billy heard the shots and ran for the back of the house.

When he got to the kitchen, he looked out the window and spotted a man working his way to the back of the house. He fired one shot through the window. The bullet struck the man and spun him around before he dropped to the ground. Billy didn't know why there weren't more men in back of the house, but he didn't care. He went out the kitchen door and started running for the river.

Clint worked his way around to the back of the house as shots rang out in front. Some of the Regulators were trying to shoot their way out in that direction, but he figured Billy would be smart and try to get out the back.

When Clint reached the back of the house, he saw a lone man back there also, then watched as the man was shot. Without hesitating, Clint turned and headed for the river.

In front of the house Alex McSween was prone on the ground, dead. Several of Billy's group, all Mexican, were also dead, as was a man named Harvey Morris. Others stood with their hands in the air, having thrown their guns to the ground.

Marion Turner went to each man in turn, grabbing him by the front of the shirt and studying him. Finally, he turned and glared at Peppin.

"He's not here!" he shouted. "Billy the Kid isn't here. Didn't anybody cover the back?"

Peppin was staring in turn at McSween's body, and looking up at the burning house.

"You had that fire started, didn't you?" he demanded of Turner.

"Something had to be done," Turner said. "Bullets were useless against the walls of the house, and the military was doing nothing. What else would work on wood better than fire?"

"Damn you," Peppin said, "there had to be another way."

"Well, you weren't comin' up with any ideas," Turner said. He turned away and shouted, "Find Billy! Check the river."

Clint reached the Rio Bonito and stopped. There was no one ahead of him, so he turned and waited. He didn't have long to wait, because Billy appeared just moments later, gun in hand. He stopped short when he saw Clint standing between him and the river.

"Adams," Billy said. "You come to stop me?"

"I came to bring you in, Billy," Clint said.

"Whataya think will happen if I let you bring me in?" Billy asked. "They'll kill me."

"I'll turn you over to Peppin."

"I'll never make it past Turner and his men," Billy said. "So I guess it's between you and me." He holstered his gun.

Clint had a decision to make. All he'd thought about was getting Billy to surrender; he hadn't considered killing him. Did he want to stop him that badly? What would this explosion of violence, these past five days, do to the situation in Lincoln? Was it the end, a new beginning, or would things just go on the way they had? And with Chisum, the man who had brought him into it, backing off, was there any point at all to his continued presence?

"Adams?" Billy asked. "We gonna do this?"

Clint looked at Billy, and he looked like dozens of young gunnies who had stood in front of him, cocky as all hell, waiting to prove themselves.

Suddenly, they both became aware that men were approaching them from the direction of the burning house.

"Make up your mind," Billy said.

Clint stood aside and said, "Go."

"What?" Billy looked shocked.

"Go on!"

Billy ran down to the river's edge, then turned and looked at Clint again.

"Why? I know you ain't afraid of me."

"I decided you're right," Clint said. "If I turn you over to them they'll kill you."

"I killed three lawmen."

"I'll think about that later," Clint said. "Now go!"

Billy plunged into the river, which at this point was not deep. He waded across to the other side, turned, stared at Clint a moment, then waved and moved off into the wood.

Clint turned to face the approaching members of the posse, already wondering if he'd done the right thing in letting Billy the Kid go.

He never saw William Bonney again.

PART FOUR

FIFTY-THREE

LINCOLN COUNTY, BACK TO THE PRESENT

What became known as the Five Day War in Lincoln County had not been the end of the violence in Lincoln County, New Mexico, but it was the end for Clint Adams. He left Lincoln the next day and had not been back to the county until he rode into White Oaks.

If Chisum was withdrawing his backing of Billy the Kid, then Clint had finally felt that he could leave. The man behind the killing of Tunstall had not been caught, but everyone seemed to know who it was. However, that hadn't become the main issue in Lincoln. The main thing everyone was talking about was bringing in Billy the Kid.

With Tunstall and McSween dead, the only other man left alive who Billy had been working for was Chisum, and the rancher turned his back on the Kid. From that day forward the Kid felt nothing but hatred for John Chisum.

Clint heard later that Pat Garrett had become the law

in Lincoln County, and still later that he'd finally tracked Billy to Fort Sumner, where he killed him.

So Billy the Kid was killed, and the incidents that occurred in Lincoln County for a period of about three years became part of history.

Billy, too, became part of history, but more in the way Wild Bill Hickok and Jesse James had. After their deaths, rumors began to emerge that they had been seen alive in certain places. Clint had been friends with both Hickok and Jesse. He, himself, had disproved at least one Hickok sighting, and he never believed the Jesse James sightings, because Jesse's own wife saw his body after he was killed.

Now, however, there had been a Billy the Kid sighting right back in Lincoln County. There were still plenty of Billy supporters in Lincoln, and if he was still alive that's the place he'd hide out.

Clint had been within riding distance of Lincoln County when he became aware of the rumor, and since he had never been back there, he decided to ride by and check it out.

He sat in the Wortley now, having experienced all the memories flooding back. Across the street was the courthouse where Billy had been held until he escaped, once again killing lawmen—two, this time. No one knew how he'd gotten ahold of a gun, but he made his escape after that shooting, only to be tracked down by Pat Garrett— in spite of the fact, they say, that Garrett and Billy had been friends. But Garrett had put on a badge, and had a job to do, and he did it.

It was years later when Clint met Garrett during the Fountain Murders, and he never discussed his own experiences in Lincoln with the man. Clint didn't like thinking about that time, because he felt he'd wasted much of it. Perhaps at this age—older, hopefully wiser—he might have reacted differently. Or maybe he would have been smart enough to stay out of it completely.

That might have been the smartest thing of all.

Clint walked the streets of Lincoln, passing the place where the McSween house had stood. Nothing new had been erected on that site, and he had lost track of Susan McSween. He walked down to the place near the river where he and Billy had faced off. What would have happened if one of them had become impatient and slapped leather? Was the Kid good enough to have outdrawn him, or would he now be known as the man who killed Billy the Kid, instead of that title going to Pat Garrett? He had enough of a reputation without having that added to it, so he was glad it was Garrett.

Walking back to the Wortley, where he'd left Eclipse, he wondered what had happened to Susan McSween, and he wondered who in town would know.

Or perhaps not in this town.

Clint rode back to White Oaks, where he was still staying. He had no desire to stay at the Wortley again. Just having a drink there and sitting on the porch had brought back vivid memories of his failures. All these years later he wondered what he could have done to prevent the death of Alex McSween and some of the others. Not Tunstall, because that happened soon after he'd arrived, but certainly Sheriff Brady and McSween and perhaps some of the other lawmen. As for Billy, there was no other way for his life to end, especially when Pat Garrett put on the Lincoln County badge.

Clint put Eclipse up in the White Oaks livery and walked over to the Little Casino. So much of Lincoln County looked unchanged, especially Belle La Mar's place. The bodies in the seats and at the bar might have been different—or some might even have been the same— but it all *looked* the same.

It was late afternoon, and as he entered he saw that the girls were out in force—including Ruby. She was standing at a table between two cowboys, talking to them, but when she saw Clint she excused herself and crossed the floor to him.

"I've been waiting for you."

"Sorry," he said, "I've been, uh, busy." Strolling down memory lane could be time-consuming.

"Too busy for me?"

"Never."

"It's early," she said, "but stick around and I'll see you tonight, after work."

"I'll be around," he said. "Is Belle around?"

"In her office, I think."

"Thanks."

Belle's office was in the same place it had been the one time he'd been in there. He walked to the door and knocked.

"Come!"

He entered and found her behind her desk.

"What a nice surprise," she said. "Did you like Ruby?"

"Very much," he said.

"Not the same type as Fiona at all."

"No," Clint said, "very different."

"That girl was kind of upset the way you left last time," she pointed out. "Not even a goodbye."

"I . . . I'd had enough of Lincoln County."

"Don't worry," she said, "I told her that was just like a man. She recovered."

"That's good."

"What brings you lookin' for me today?"

"I wanted to ask you a question," Clint said. "I figure you know everything that goes on in this county."

"A lot," she said, "but not everything." Still, it was clear that she was flattered. "What can I tell you?"

"Susan McSween," he said. "What happened to her after the death of her husband? Where did she go?"

"Where did she go?" Belle asked. "She never went anywhere. She still lives right here in Lincoln County, Clint."

FIFTY-FOUR

According to Belle La Mar, Susan McSween was now Susan McSween Barber. She had remarried four years after her husband's death, and she and her new husband had a spread at Three Rivers, about sixty miles southwest of Lincoln.

Clint rode out to the Three Rivers spread, unsure of what he would say to Susan when he saw her. The death of her husband was one of his failures, after all. Still, he felt compelled to ride out and see her.

The ranch was nothing like John Chisum's spread had been, but it was impressive just the same. Clint was met by several ranch hands as he rode up to the house and asked for Mrs. Barber.

"Who wants her?" someone asked.

He turned in his saddle to look behind him and was surprised by what he saw.

"Well, I'll be," he said.

Approaching him on foot was Sweet Johnny Boggs,

older but still possessing that smile, which he exhibited now.

"Hello, Clint."

"You know this guy, Boss?" one of the hands asked. "He says he wants to talk to the boss's wife."

"I know him, Zeke," Boggs said. "This is an old friend of mine, Clint Adams."

"Clint . . . Adams?" Zeke repeated. "You mean . . . The Gunsmith?"

He and the other men looked suitably impressed, but Boggs gave them no time for hero worship.

"Get back to work," Boggs said. "I'll take care of our guest."

The men backed off, but didn't walk away immediately until Boggs gave them a hard look.

"Look at this horse," Boggs said, as Clint dismounted. "Where do you find them?"

"This one was a gift."

"Ride that huge gelding into the ground, did you?"

"Put him out to pasture," Clint said. "He deserved it."

The two men shook hands warmly.

"Been a while," Boggs said.

"Eight, ten years," Clint said.

"About that. What brings you here?" Then Boggs realized. "The rumors?"

"I've heard them."

"Just rumors," Boggs said. "Billy's not alive, Clint."

Clint shrugged and said, "I was in the neighborhood."

"And thought you'd come visit Mrs. Barber?"

"I didn't know she was Mrs. Barber," Clint said, "but yes, that's about it."

"Did you stop in White Oaks? Looking to play any poker while you're here?"

"I could be persuaded."

"Well, let me talk to the lady of the house and see if she wants to talk to you."

They walked toward the house together. "I won't be surprised if she says no. She wasn't too happy with me the last time I saw her."

"Then you better wait right here while I go inside and ask."

"How did you end up working for her, anyway?" Clint asked. "What happened to Chisum?"

Boggs shrugged and said, "He just wasn't the same after all . . . that happened. Wait here."

Boggs went into the house, and was gone several minutes. Clint could see that the men who had "greeted" him still had not gone very far. They were studying him from the corral. He wondered what they expected to see.

When the front door opened, Clint looked around. Boggs waved him over to the door.

"The lady will see you now," he said. "Follow me."

Boggs took Clint to a well-furnished living room. An older, more matronly Susan McSween was waiting for him there. Her body had filled out some, but her skin was still as flawless as he remembered. Briefly, the memory of her standing in his room with her beautiful breasts bared came to him, and she colored slightly, as if she could read his mind.

"Clint Adams," she said. "How nice to see you after all this time. Come in. Sit down."

"I wasn't sure you'd feel that way, Mrs. Barber."

"It's still Susan," she said. "Thank you, Johnny."

Boggs nodded and withdrew.

"How did you find me?" she asked.

"I rode into White Oaks, asked around."

"Madam Varnish is the only one who knows everything that goes on around here."

"That's true."

"Must have been a surprise for you to see Johnny here, as well."

"Yes, it was. And your husband?"

"Away on business, I'm afraid," she said, "not that he does that much around here."

Obviously, she was not happy with her marriage.

"Can I offer you a drink? I have some brandy here that my husband brought back from San Francisco."

"Are you having any?"

"Yes."

"Then I'll have some."

She walked to a sideboard and poured two glass tumblers from as crystal decanter. He noticed that she dressed in the same style—high-necked, formfitting—but more expensively. The weight she had added was not unattractive. For a woman in her forties, she was still desirable.

She approached him and handed him a glass.

"To old friends."

"Susan," he said, "before I drink to that toast—"

"Clint," she said, cutting him off, "I realized soon after you left Lincoln that you had no more control over what was happening than I did. That Alex was killed was not your fault." She lifted her glass. "To old friends?"

"To old friends," he said. He drank from the tumbler, looking down into it.

"And to unfinished business," Susan added.

"What do you mea—" he started, looking up, but he stopped short when he saw her.

She was standing in the center of the living room with her dress down around her waist. Her breasts had filled out over the years, becoming even larger, sagging slightly from their weight. They were still breathtaking, though— full, round, with large pink nipples.

"Susan—"

"I was embarrassed and ashamed that day in your room," she said, "when you rejected me, but I've always wondered . . ."

"Susan . . . ," he said again, his mouth dry despite the fact he'd just drank some brandy.

"Are you going to reject me again, Clint Adams?"

He might have, but at that moment she did something surprisingly wanton. She slid her hands beneath her breasts, cupping them, and then gently rubbed her thumbs over her nipples.

"Hell, no," he rasped.

FIFTY-FIVE

They kissed standing in the center of the living room. Clint pushed her hands down to her sides so he could cup her full breasts, enjoying the weight of them in his hands. When his thumbs touched her nipples they were hard, and she moaned into his mouth. She couldn't have known he was coming, and yet she smelled fresh and sweet, as if she'd come right from a bath.

When they broke the kiss she said, "Well, that was a long time in coming."

"Susan—"

"No talking," she said, "at least not by you. Come with me."

She took his hand and led him from the living room, down a hallway to a bedroom in the back of the house.

"I don't want to use your husband's—"

"Hush," she said, pressing a hand to his lips. "We have separate bedrooms. His is upstairs, and mine is here. And there is no one in the house but you and me."

She kissed him again, this time putting one hand behind his head and pulling toward her. She put her tongue into his mouth as far as it would go, and the kiss went on for a very long time. He slid his hands down her back until he was cupping the cheeks of her ass, and pulling her tightly against him.

"Oh my," she said, when she felt the erection through his pants. "Did you have one of those back then? That night in your room?"

"Oh, yes."

"And did your little friend from White Oaks help you with it?"

"Not that night."

"Good," she said, "then I'll consider this leftover from that night. That makes it mine."

She slipped out of her dress and then, naked, dropped to her knees in front of him. She helped him off with his boots, then undid trousers and pulled them and his shorts down around his ankles. His erection, hard and pulsing, sprang out at her and she said, "Oh," and then took it in both hands.

"How very nice," she said. She licked it, wetting it thoroughly and moaning through her enjoyment, and then—when it was so wet it felt cold—she slipped it into her hot mouth. She rode him that way, holding him at the base of his penis with one hand, fondling his heavy balls with the other, and sucking him avidly. She bobbed her head up and down on him until she was making wet sucking and popping sounds as he sometimes slipped completely from her mouth. It surprised him that she was every bit as good at this as the other blonde who worked for Madam Varnish, Ruby. But then he forgot about that and just surrendered himself to the sensations she was causing with her mouth and her hands . . .

When he was as hard as a railroad spike—or so it seemed—she stood, took hold of him and tugged him to the bed. She tossed the bedcovers completely off of it and pulled him down to the bed with her, him on top.

"I can't wait anymore," she said. "I'll play with you some more later, but I want you in me right now!"

She spread her legs wide open for him. He knelt between them, touched the head of his penis to her wet pussy, and then slid it in gently.

"Ooh, my god" she groaned, "yessss. So that's what I've been waiting all these years for!"

She sounded completely shocked.

She explained to him later that she had been married twice and neither of her husbands was a very good lover.

"And you never took a lover outside your marriage to find out what you were missing?"

"I never even thought about it until you . . . until you came to Lincoln. From the moment I saw you in my husband's store I thought about you . . . that way. And then that night in your room . . . well, I thought I'd die if you didn't take me . . . and you didn't."

"And you didn't die."

"No," she said, "but I wanted you even more after that, and it made me feel ashamed. My god, I was in my thirties and I acted like a schoolgirl. I should have just grabbed you and made you fuck me!"

Her hand flew to her mouth then, proving that there was still some of the schoolgirl in her.

She snuggled into his arms and said, "See how wanton you've made me? I have no shame anymore."

They laid that way in silence for a while and then she asked, "Is it always like that?"

"Like what?"

"So . . . wonderful," she said. "It was like . . . fire in my . . . down there, and flashing lights in my head . . ."

"Well," he said, "I don't know if it's like that every time for the woman. It is for me, though."

"Then you're very lucky. I've missed so much, I suppose, but somehow I knew you'd come back here."

"So you've been . . . waiting for me?"

"I suppose," she said. "Yes, I guess I have been waiting for you to come back and be my lover . . . even if it's only for one day."

"Susan . . . that's a big responsibility."

"Oh," she said, reaching down between his legs and fondling him until he was hard, "I rather think you're up to it."

FIFTY-SIX

Later they sat up together in the bed, leaning back against the expensive wooden headboard. The light coming in the window was fading and Clint was worried.

"What are your men going to think?" he asked. "And Johnny. What's he going to think?"

"I don't care." She shrugged. "Maybe they'll think I got a visit from an old friend and we've been talking all this time."

"What about your husband—"

"You're worrying too much, Clint," she said. "I'm not worried, so don't you be. Okay?"

He hesitated, then said. "Okay."

She clutched the sheet to her throat, covering her breasts and shoulders, and asked, "So why did you really come here?"

"To Lincoln County? The rumors."

"About Billy?"

"That's right."

"You think he's alive?"

"I think he's not supposed to be alive," Clint said. "Pat Garrett said he killed him. I've met Garrett since then, and I'm inclined to believe him. Except . . ."

"Except what?"

"Well, weren't they supposed to be friends, at one point?"

She nodded and said, "Big Casino, and Little Casino."

"What?"

"That's what they called each other.

"They were close enough to have nicknames for each other?"

"Apparently so."

"Then . . . what if Garrett helped fake Billy's death?"

"Why would Billy come back here, so many years later?" she asked. "And make no attempt to disguise himself?"

"I don't—wait. How do you know he's not making an attempt to hide himself?"

"He's wearing the same clothes," she said.

"Which clothes?"

"That stupid black hat, the vest . . . the clothes he's wearing in the photo."

Clint sat straight up.

"How do you know what he's wearing, Susan?"

"Well . . . I've seen him." She looked away.

"You've . . . what?"

"I've seen him," she said, and then looked at him. "I've seen Billy the Kid—or his ghost."

Clint suggested they get out of bed, get dressed and go back into the living room. He couldn't concentrate, lying in bed naked with her. Besides, he still felt badly sleeping with another man's wife, even though she said they weren't happy.

"Tell me this again," he said, when they were in the living room with a glass of brandy each. A glance at the

clock on the mantel told him he'd been there three hours.
"You think you've seen Billy's ghost?"

"I said I've seen Billy, or his ghost," she said. "That's
what I said."

"Have you told anyone?"

"Not until I told you just now."

"Not even your husband?"

"No one."

"But why not?"

"Because they'd be looking at me just the way you are,
right now," she replied. "Like I'm crazy."

"Susan, I'm sorry if that's how I'm looking at you,
but . . . tell me, when did you see him? And where?"

"Here and there," she said. "He just sort of . . . pops out
and stares at me, sometimes from a distance, sometimes
from closer."

"Has he ever been . . . in the house?"

"No," she said. "Never."

"So he hasn't walked through walls, or anything?"

She looked away and set her glass down on a nearby
table.

"Now you're making fun of me."

"No, I'm not," he said, "I'm trying to understand. Do
you think you've really seen Billy, or a ghost?"

"Well . . . I haven't ever been close enough to see if
he's, you know, older? He's wearing pretty much what he
used to wear, but . . ." She trailed off.

"Have you heard of anyone else seeing what you've
seen?"

"Oh yes," she said. "Just because I don't talk about it
doesn't mean other folks don't. Lots of people claim to
have seen him."

"Where?" Clint asked. "Tell me where."

"Are you going to look for him?"

"If this is some phony playing on Billy's reputation,
then yes, I want to find him."

"Why?"

"Because I've had people do this to friends of mine before."

"But . . . Billy wasn't your friend," she pointed out.

"It doesn't matter," Clint said. "The dead deserve more respect than that, don't you think?"

She stared at him for a moment, then said, "As a matter of fact, I do."

FIFTY-SEVEN

Susan told Clint that "Billy" had often been seen in White Oaks, outside the Little Casino, and in Lincoln, around the site of the old McSween mansion. In the time Clint had been there he had seen nothing, but when he left Susan's he intended to go back to White Oaks and ask around.

Outside the house he ran into Johnny Boggs again.

"Uh, lots of catching up—" he started, but Boggs waved away his explanation.

"You don't have to explain anything to me, Clint," he said.

"Johnny . . . have you seen Billy around here?"

"No," Boggs said, "whether he's real or a ghost, I haven't seen him myself."

"Do you believe others have?"

"I believe they believe they have. What are you going to do?"

"I'm just going to nose around some," Clint said. "See what I can find out."

"You think it's an impostor?"

"Seems more likely than a ghost, don't you think?"

Boggs shrugged and said, "With Billy, who knows?"

Clint returned to White Oaks and Belle La Mar's place. He stood at the bar, had a few beers and listened to conversations going on around him. It reminded him of his first few days there, all those years ago. Then he'd been waiting to pick up bits of information about the Lincoln County trouble that had been going on. Now he was just listening to see if anyone mentioned Billy the Kid.

And the name did come up, several times, but never in the context he was interested in. It seemed that folks had not forgotten the Lincoln County War and still took sides—some Tunstall-McSween's, some Murphy-Dolan-Riley's, but more often than not they were taking the side of Billy the Kid. And most of those thought that Pat Garrett was a dirty, no-good traitor to Billy, for shooting him down that way.

Then one voice asked, "Do you think he really shot him?"

Eyes turned to the speaker, including Clint's. He appeared to be in his late twenties, and he was standing at the end of the bar by himself, holding a beer.

"Whataya mean?" someone replied. "Everybody knows Garrett killed Billy."

"You ain't been listenin' to the rumors, have ya?" somebody else asked.

"That's hogwash," a third man said. "Billy's dead."

"Maybe he ain't," the first man said.

"I heard he'd been seen around," the stranger said. "Hasn't anyone seen him?"

Clint listened closely, glad he didn't have to ask these questions himself.

"I ain't seen him," a man said, "but I seen his ghost."

"There ain't no such thing as ghosts."

"Yeah, tell that to Billy . . ."

The stranger seemed satisfied with the direction the conversation had taken and subsided, leaning over his beer. Clint watched the man while an argument ensued about whether or not Billy the Kid's ghost had come to Lincoln County.

Clint had taken a table and was nursing a beer when Johnny Boggs came walking into the Little Casino. He spotted Clint, grabbed a beer from the bar and walked over.

"Mind if I join you?"

"Have a seat," Clint said, "but first take a look at that fella standing at the end of the bar.

Boggs sneaked a peek then sat down.

"What about him?"

"Know him?"

"Boggs turned and looked again. "Can't say I do. What about him?"

"He seems as interested in the Billy the Kid story as I am," Clint said. "And he seems to be about the same age Billy would be now."

Boggs turned and looked a third time.

"You think he could be Billy?"

"If Billy wasn't dead."

"You're sure he's dead?"

"As sure as I can be without having seen the body."

"Then you believe the ghost story?"

"It's more likely somebody's looking for attention by impersonating Billy."

"And you're going to find him?"

"I'm going to take a look around."

"So I guess that means no poker?"

"Not this trip."

Boggs shrugged and drank his beer.

"Why'd you stay around, Johnny?" Clint asked. "Why didn't you leave?"

"I'm not like you, Clint," Boggs said. "Being in one place for a long period of time doesn't spook me. All I need is a job and I'm happy."

"Well," Clint said, "if you see any ghosts you'll let me know, huh?"

"You'll be the first."

FIFTY-EIGHT

Clint waited for Ruby to finish work and took her back to his hotel with him. He rediscovered the lush curves of her body by undressing her slowly.

"I guess you like big women," she said as he lifted her breasts to his mouth.

"Actually," he said, "I love all women."

She cradled his head to her breasts and said, "Lucky women . . ."

Later she asked, "How much longer will you be in town?"

"I guess that depends on when I can find Billy the Kid's ghost," he answered.

"And where are you going to look? Here in White Oaks?"

"No," Clint said, "most of the sightings seem to have been in Lincoln. I'll go there and see what I can find."

"Will you stay in a hotel there?"

"No," he said, "I spent enough time in a hotel there years ago. I'll continue to stay here."

"Well," she said, snuggling up to him, "that's good for me."

Still later she woke him.

"Again?" he asked.

"No," she said, "I feel bad."

"About what?"

"Something I didn't tell you."

"And what was that?" he asked, with his eyes still closed.

"Something I heard about . . . you know, the ghost." She lowered her voice to a whisper.

He opened one eye, looked at her and asked, "What about the ghost?"

"I know where he's been seen the most times . . ."

She hadn't wanted to tell him at first, because he might leave too soon, but then she'd felt guilty about keeping it from him. After she told him, they went back to sleep and slept until morning. She had breakfast with him in the hotel dining room and then she went back to her room and he went to the livery to saddle Eclipse.

The next day Clint was back at the Rio Bonito, fifty feet from where the McSween house had stood, the last place he'd seen Billy the Kid. He walked around until he thought he'd found the exact spot where he'd been standing. The river was higher now than it had been then, but he thought he'd found the right spot.

Ruby had told him that most of the people who claimed to have seen Billy the Kid said they'd seen him by the river behind where the McSween house had been. That was real exact for him, and much too much of a coincidence. He had the feeling that she was sending him here for a reason.

As if on cue a man stepped from behind a tree. He was standing almost where Billy had stood that day.

"Adams."

Clint saw that it was the same man who had been standing at the end of the bar the night before, the one who was the right age to be Billy, if he was still alive. He was wearing a dark brown leather vest over a lighter brown shirt, and a brown flat-brimmed hat.

"Where are the clothes?" Clint asked. "And the hat."

"I don't need them today."

"Just to make people think they were seeing Billy, huh?"

He was the same size that Billy had been, perhaps slightly heavier.

"You don't think I'm Billy Bonney?"

"Billy's dead, killed by Pat Garrett."

"What if I told you that you were wrong? That Billy wasn't killed that day?"

"I wouldn't believe you."

"If I'm not Billy," the man said, "then how did I know to have the girl send you here? The last place you saw him?"

"I'm betting that during the time that Billy was on the run, after the McSween house was burned, he ran into you. Maybe you and he got along because you were the same age. Anyway, he told you about facing me here, and how I let him go. That's my guess."

The man stared at him for a few moments, then shook his head and said, "That's a good guess. Yes, sir, that's a mighty good guess."

"Why come to Lincoln and impersonate Billy?" Clint asked.

"I said it was a good guess," the man said. "I didn't say it was right."

"What's your name?"

"I'm going by Harry Antrim, at the moment."

Antrim. The name meant nothing to Clint.

"Okay, you're Harry Antrim," Clint said, "but are you still claiming to be Billy the Kid?"

"Well," Antrim said, with a crooked smile, "I ain't no kid—not no more."

Clint had been face to face with Billy twice. Once in the McSween house when he tried to talk him into giving himself up, and once right here by the river. For the life of him, though, he couldn't say whether or not this man was Billy the Kid all grown up. Could have been—then again, might not be.

"Okay," Clint said, "Harry Antrim or Billy, why did you have Ruby send me out here?"

"Ain't she somethin'?" Antrim asked. "I ain't never been with a gal like her before—big as her, I mean. She's a might bigger than I am, but she's stuck on me for some reason. She'd do just about anything I ask her to."

"Like sending me out here," Clint said. She was a good little actress, all right, playing all guilty and finally telling him where to find "Billy." "But why? That's my question. Why'd you want me here?"

"This is a place where you have some unfinished business," Antrim said.

"With you?"

"With Billy the Kid," the man said. "This is where you last saw him, right?"

"That's right."

"Face to face, you two *pistoleros*," the man said, laughing.

"Right again."

"And you let him go."

"Yes."

"Why?"

"Lots of reasons," Clint said, "one of which he and I discussed before he ran off. If you're him, then you'd remember."

"It wasn't because you were afraid of him?"

"No."

The man seemed to take umbrage at the fact that Clint answered so quickly.

"Not even a little?"

"No."

"Why not?"

"Because," Clint said, "if he had touched his gun I would have killed him."

The man shifted his feet and frowned.

"You're sure of that."

"Yes."

"Goddamn," Antrim said, "you're the surest man—"

"What are you doing here, Mr. Antrim?" Clint asked, cutting him off.

"Well, you was lookin' for the Ghost of Billy the Kid, wasn't you?" the man asked. "You at least gotta admit I'm that. Here, look."

Clint tensed as the man moved back into the trees, then came out and tossed the Billy the Kid clothes and hat into the dirt. From the best of Clint's recollection the hat looked pretty authentic. Black pants and black vest—well, black was black.

"There's your ghost."

"I don't understand," Clint said, "what dressing as Billy and allowing yourself to be seen accomplished."

"Well," Harry Antrim said, with great satisfaction, "it got you here, didn't it?"

FIFTY-NINE

"No," Clint said, "that's not it."

Antrim raised his eyebrows.

"There's no way you could have known I was in the area," Clint went on. "This could not have been staged for my benefit."

"Well," Antrim said, "not you specifically, but The Gunsmith is a bigger catch than I anticipated."

"You mean you were just . . . fishing for . . . anybody?"

"Not just anybody," the man said. "Just somebody with a rep, somebody who couldn't resist looking for Billy the Kid's ghost."

Coincidence, Clint thought, he hated coincidence. So he just happened to be riding near Lincoln County, just happened to hear the rumor, just happened to have a history here in Lincoln County . . .

"Adams."

Clint looked at Antrim.

"What's it matter to you whether I'm Billy the Kid or

not?" the man asked. "You'll be dead in minutes—maybe even seconds."

"You're that sure of yourself?"

The man who may or may not have been Billy the Kid grinned. "I'm dead sure."

"Now, wait a minute," Clint said. "I still don't buy this—"

"I ain't got the time to convince you," Antrim said. "You're finally gonna have your showdown with Billy the Kid."

It looked like the mystery was not going to be solved. This was one of the times Clint was not going to get a logical explanation for things that had happened. He was here, this Antrim fella was here, and it was coming down to this.

"You're not Billy," Clint said. "You can't be."

"Why not?"

"Because Billy wouldn't do this."

"No more talk."

Antrim—or Billy—or whoever he was—went for his gun, and Clint could see immediately that the man had good reason to be cocksure. He was fast—damn fast! He even managed to clear leather before Clint drilled him dead center, one bullet to the chest. The impact knocked him back a few steps and then he went down, his gun falling from his hand.

Clint walked up to the fallen man and kicked his gun farther away from him before leaning over. There was blood leaking from his mouth and he was going fast. He barely had time to say, "Goddamn, that was fast!" before the light in his eyes went out and he was dead.

He'd been fast, all right—but he still wasn't Billy the Kid.

Sheriff Dave Eidson crouched over the body, then stood up straight and looked at Clint.

"What makes you think he ain't Billy the Kid?" Eidson asked.

"You ever see Billy the Kid, Sheriff?" Clint asked.

"No, just in pictures."

"Well, I've seen him, and that isn't him."

"You're sure."

"I'm sure," Clint said. "Pat Garrett killed Billy the Kid in Fort Sumner."

"You know your Billy the Kid history, huh?"

"Pretty well," Clint said. "I was here during the Lincoln County conflict—or the 'War' as some call it."

"Well," Eidson said, "I'll get some men to carry him into town to the undertaker's."

"That's fine."

"You gonna pay to bury him?"

"I guess so," Clint said. "After all, I killed him."

"What'd he say his name was?"

"Antrim, Harry Antrim."

Eidson stared at Clint a moment.

"What?" Clint asked.

"You say you're up on your Billy the Kid history?"

"Pretty much."

"And the name Antrim don't mean nothin' to you?" the man asked, "Harry Antrim?"

Clint thought a moment, then said, "No, why?"

"Antrim was the name of the man Billy's mother married after his father died," Eidson said, "and Billy's real middle name was Harrison."

The lawman looked down at the dead man. "Harry Antrim."

Clint looked down, squinted at the dead man's face, then shook his head and said, "That just means this fella knew his Billy history better than I did."

Eidson looked at Clint and said, "Maybe so . . . maybe so."

The sheriff started back up toward town to fetch some

men to carry the body to the undertaker's office. Clint moved around so he could look at the dead man from another angle.

He thought back to that day in the McSween house, when Billy had looked so determined, and then five days later, right down here at the water's edge. In his mind he tried to see both faces—young Billy's, and this man's—side by side.

Finally he shook his head and said, "No, huh-uh . . . no . . . I don't know who you really were, Mr. Harry Antrim, but you were not Billy the Kid."

Clint started to walk after the sheriff, turned, said, "No," once more, then continued on and did not look back again.

AUTHOR'S NOTE

Most of the incidents in this book are true and quite well documented in both books and movies. These accounts are, of course, fictionalized. Certain things were changed for the author's convenience, but most of all the incidents of the so-called "Five Day War." In this account only Alex McSween and his wife, Susan, were in the house with Billy and his men. In reality, there were other adults in the house, as well as the McSween's four children. However, for reasons all my own I did not want to deal with the logistics of placing the children, so I left them out.

I'd like to thank the residents of Lincoln and DeBaca Counties in New Mexico for their hospitality while I was there researching Billy and the Lincoln County War.

J. R. ROBERTS
THE
GUNSMITH

**Explore the exciting Old West with one
of the men who made it wild!**

JAKE LOGAN
TODAY'S HOTTEST ACTION WESTERN!